First edition independently printed 2024.
This edition printed 2024 by Pope Lick Press.

DEREK HEATH

PARLIAMENT OF WITCHES

POPE LICK PRESS

2024

ROPE

Orange light spotted the windscreen where beads of condensation had dried into iridescent flakes. A bloated afternoon sun baked the roof of the 1984 Tasmin, the wedge-shaped keel of the bonnet frying softly as the car cruised along the chipped throat of the road. The two-seater was uncomfortably warm inside, even with the windows rolled down. Usually Tilley would have pushed the old sports car to its limit on a straight, quiet road like this one, but for the past half-hour he had been disturbed by a frequent and juddering rattle beneath the chassis and was reluctant to drive at more than forty. He admired the scenery with some hesitation as he navigated the old road: thick verges punched up from the cracked edges of the tarmac, and beyond scraggly late-summer hedgerows the fields were tall and crowing for harvest. Wind blew distant bony trees and deep orange banks of cloud rolled into the clutches of faint, pink fingers scrabbling over the horizon.

Tilley glanced occasionally at the road map splayed open on the passenger seat. The tattered corner of the page fluttered weakly.

Laying across a faded knot of red A-roads, reeking of fruity putrefaction despite the clear sandwich bag it was sealed in, was a severed hand.

The fingers were curled and thin, the hand itself so shrivelled and grey it looked mummified. It might have been, at one point, but any spices and gauze had been worn to nothing by time and all that was left of the thing were knobs of crusty grey bone and the clotted tendons of dust that held them together.

Jonathan Tilley had driven in silence for most of the journey. The radio was busted, and besides that he preferred the quiet to most things they played nowadays. Sometimes he would listen to modern music – Abe had introduced him to The Temperance Movement recently, and he quite liked them – but mostly the CDs in the glovebox were old Beatles records and the odd 70s album. He had Fleetwood Mac and Marvin Gaye in there somewhere, and the player itself contained a scratched copy of Kate Bush's *The Kick Inside*. He seldom listened to music before a job; only after, when the thing was done.

It always seemed… *wrong*, filling his head with noise before doing what he had to do. Tilley's line of work required focus, mindfulness, sobriety. Not distraction.

He swallowed as he turned the TVR around a tight bend and entered a thick tunnel of woodland. The action made his cheeks bulge with tight knots. He had lost most of his hair by sixty-five and, in the last couple of years, made the decision to shave his head entirely bald. It was far from smooth, however; the back of his cranium peppered with tiny raised bumps of scar tissue that spread up to the dome, and thin veins throbbed at his temples like cables pumped full of fluid. More scar tissue on his cheek and around his left eye, though the patterning here was different: rather than the dozens of white, fleshy mounds scattering his skull, the pale stripes exploding from the socket were ragged, like splinters through glass, punched outward from the central point of his pupil. His jaw was stubbled, many of the bristles a bright shining white, only some having retained the rusty copper colour of his hair. The deepest and freshest scars were those that raked the shelf of his jaw, from Adam's apple to chin: three thick, purplish ridges of skin had sealed over but remained largely unhealed. Claw marks.

Something vibrated in his shirt pocket and he lifted his foot off the accelerator, glancing into the rearview to check the road was clear behind him before slipping his fingers into the pocket and withdrawing his phone. He answered without taking his eyes off the road, finding the speaker button with his thumb. Normally he wouldn't have answered at all, but the Agency had said they'd call when he was due to arrive. He had stopped for a drink and to vomit in the Welcome Break toilets an hour back, accounting for the delay. Still, he must be close now.

There had been blood in the vomit again.

"Tilley," he said, his voice sombre and gravelly, like his teeth were rolling over each other in his mouth as he spoke. He tossed the phone onto the passenger seat. "Nearly there."

"ETA?" said the woman at the other end of the line. There was no greeting, no introduction. He knew the voice, though: Elena Fox had been running the BWFA for the last thirty years or so. Tilley was aware that receiving his assignments straight from the director was a privilege, but he rarely thought of her as anything but The Voice On The Phone. How could he, when he had never met the woman?

"Thirty minutes," Tilley said, peeling the car steadily around another bend and out of the woods. The hedgerows here were sparse and through them he saw thick green stalks. Directly ahead, the road began to slope downward, snaking into a valley which bent and wound toward the sea, eventually rising again to a noose of pale, cracked grey. The valley was walled by two steep, sloping cliffs: on the left, a forest of black, burnt pine screamed up turgid trenches of soil; on the right, a rise of blasted stone formed a ragged grey mouth, the boulder-toothed slackjaw of a semi-detonated quarry. The valley between was smudged with flint-walled buildings. He saw, in the middle of a huddle of vague black shapes, the tower of a small, thatched church. "I can see the village now."

"Sure this is the place?" Elena said.

Tilley clamped his teeth together, glancing briefly into the passenger seat. Beside the mobile, the severed hand twitched gently in its bag. He leaned over and poked the thing, and after a moment it twitched again, more violently this time.

As he turned his eyes back to the windscreen, the bony knotted thing flexed its fingers and wriggled, small clouds of dust falling from the withered joints as they rolled over each other. When he looked down again, it was pointing with a gnarled index finger, the tip of which was sharp and black. It tapped three times, bones clicking inside the rustling sandwich bag.

Jonathan Tilley had circled the village on the map, of course, scrawling in the same red biro he always used; still, it never hurt to have confirmation. The hand was pointing at the small village of Black Rope, a small cluster of faint grey shapes on the map surrounded by nothing for miles but patches of green.

"Mikey's sure," he said. "That's good enough for me."

"This is a big one," Elena said. "We need it neutralised, Jack. If you need extra hands—"

"I've got your number," Tilley said.

"Good man. Be careful. This book, Jack—"

"I know."

"Here if you need me. Good luck."

"Boss," Tilley grunted, reaching down to snap the phone closed. She was right: this was a big one, even for the Agency. But Tilley wasn't worried about the book. It was never the book – or the staff, or sceptre, or dead man's switch – it was the person whose possession the damn thing

(*damned thing*)

had fallen into.

In the passenger seat the severed hand had gone still again, tiny particles of dust drifting to the bottom of the sandwich bag as it settled.

"Fucking witches," Tilley said, and he squeezed the accelerator. The 1984 TVR Tasmin rattled a little as it approached Black Rope.

Tilley pulled the car onto the verge about two miles out of the village – and a little too close, for his liking, to the gnarly scaffolding of a gargantuan roadside sycamore. One day he would forget the awful image seared onto his brain in '82: the Carver boy, swinging slowly by his neck from a thick knotted branch eight feet off the ground, the boy himself only half that height. One of his plimsolls lay half-enclosed in the roots below, claimed by them. There had been a necklace of bones and crumbling beaks around his throat. His sock was damp and dripping.

The old man tumbled out of the car and into the verge, almost folding in half as he clamped an arm to his stomach. Nausea swelled up from his abdomen and punched into the roof of his mouth, making his head swim. He threw up into the grass, a little spraying the toe of his left brogue. Anyone driving by would have kept driving: the sight of a near-seventy-year-old man in a tweed jacket, with bony knees and legs like kebab skewers, chucking red-streaked bile into the verge might, in fact, have encouraged anyone driving by to speed up a little.

Throat sore, Tilley stood up straight with some difficulty and gazed at the tree. The branches were bare

(the creaking of the rope as the poor Carver boy swung to and fro, his head lolling forward, the dark blossoms across his stomach signifying that perhaps he had been dead before his neck was broken)

and the thick, long-indulged roots had pushed up pebbled dunes of tarmac and formed a cracked mess of black at the edge of the road. The sycamore was ancient. Wheezing a little – trying not to put too much strain on his torn oesophagus – Tilley wiped his lips on the back of a nobbled hand and stalked to the tree, leaning heavily on it. He clutched his stomach with one hand and stared quietly down into the valley.

Black Rope was scattered like hunks of debris between the slope of dark forest and the blasted rock bulwark, each hillside tumbling down into the valley like an approaching army storming the tiny place. The soldiers – those tall, infinitely mottled pines, each one a scar of black scored down the pinkening horizon, and a battalion of rolling stones dragging white streaks down the bulwark – would find nothing down there to loot or pillage or fuck or whatever it was they planned to do; the village looked empty.

Desolate.

The central hub of a round-towered church seemed to have been jettisoned directly out from somewhere beneath the crust of the earth, catching itself in knots of root and fallen trunks as it breached the surface. In fact many of the little flint buildings surrounding it, too, were overgrown with ivy and tangled walls of thicket. There were no roads down there, only dirt tracks connecting grey-rooved bungalows to grey-rooved cottages, and those to a crescent of grey-rooved terraces. He saw smoke drilling faintly from the chimney of what looked like an inn, and at the distant reaches of the village a building with a large yard that might have been a schoolhouse. He saw a smudge of green that might have been a park; a few glints of metal, burnt specks of dust in the sunlight, that must have been parked cars. Heard a bicycle bell as if through water.

There was life down there, but that life was dull and subdued. Quiet.

Too quiet, he almost felt like saying. What a cliché. But wasn't that just him, now? Wasn't he just another walking cliché? Why not embrace it, like he'd embraced the stomach cancer and the drinking and the loneliness of life?

"Listen to yourself," he muttered, and pinned his focus on a small building near the church, a chapel or vicarage of some kind, the roof cluttered with moss, the tiny spots of the windows dark and uninviting.

The book was somewhere down there, he knew it. Michael knew it. He could *feel* it.

As he turned away from the tree and headed back for the car, he thought

(*it's not real it's not* now)

he heard rope creaking. There was a darkness in Black Rope, and the darkness had its hands on that book. Tilley had experience of witches, and Elena was right. This was a big one. The book was old, and powerful, and he could feel its shadowy fingers clawing at him even out here. And the witch herself…

she must have been powerful, perhaps more so than he was equipped to deal with. Witches were awful creatures, many of them impossibly old and dreadfully wizened, most having long since abandoned their humanity – what little they might have possessed – for power and malice. Tilley steeled himself and slid into the car.

Whatever he was about to find here… he was certain it was crueller and more repugnant than anything he'd faced before.

CATCH DOG

April moved quickly down the centre aisle, heading for the freezers at the back of the store. She hummed quietly as she moved, hands in the pockets of her oversized coat, Taylor Swift's latest album pumping gently into her brain through the earphones snaking up through her shirt. As she passed a bay of soup cans, a lanky shop assistant looked up from the shelf he was stacking and smiled politely in her direction. The girl smiled back.

She was eighteen, five-foot-six, dressed in loose black jeans and a baggy orange blouse. The scarf around her neck was hand-knitted; the coat was her father's. *Had been* her father's. She moved quietly despite her clunky, rubber-soled boots, the brown leather worn in and softened through years of use. As she reached the freezers she glanced back to make sure the shop assistant wasn't watching her. He had migrated to the trolley standing in the middle of the aisle and was preparing to wheel it back toward the till point at the other end of the store. For a second she watched him checking his trolley, a pang of guilt twisting in her gut. Then she turned back to the freezer, slid open the door, and reached in.

Slipping a couple things into the pocket of her dad's coat, April moved into the last aisle, mouthing along to "Snow on the Beach" as she dipped a hand into the refrigerator and grabbed a slim pack of mushrooms. These quickly went into the coat's inside pocket, joining a pack of pitta (she needed bread, but loaves were too big to shoplift and the packaging for the tortilla wraps rustled too much) and a can of peas that thumped awkwardly against her breast as she crossed the rest of the store. As she reached the end of the aisle she stepped into the field of view of a ceiling-mounted security camera – one of four – and reached for a block of cheese, pausing for a moment with it in her hand as if checking the label. Making a show of deciding against it, she reached back to the shelf to return it – and deftly slipped it into her sleeve.

When she was halfway across the store, she slipped

her hand into her pocket. The block of cheese dropped in nicely. She moved toward the front doors, nodding her thanks to the shop assistant, now behind the till. He nodded back. She had seen him a few times now and wondered if he might be growing suspicious. She'd have to find another store to add to her rotation.

Resisting the urge to look up at the security camera above the door, she stepped out into the warm afternoon air and glanced back. Her reflection in the storefront window looked furtively back at her, dark eyes hidden beneath her messy fringe. Her thick, brown hair hadn't been washed in a couple of days, but it didn't yet appear greasy. Her eyes were ringed with red. She swallowed, looked away, then reached into her jeans to turn up the music on her phone and started the lonely three-mile walk back to Black Rope.

The clouds broiled with the sizzling light of evening as Tilley drove into town, cruising slowly past a small doctor's surgery on the left and what looked like a communal recycling point on the right. The tarmac was blistered and pale, the pavements crumbling. As he turned onto a small terraced street he watched a light blink off on the second floor of a squat grey house; across from it, a young woman slipped out of a parked Astra and offered him a friendly wave. He supplied a three-fingered signal over the wheel and a curt smile in return, gently pushing the TVR to the end of the street. The woman stooped through an ivy-tangled arbour and disappeared into her front lawn. He passed a postbox with a crocheted octopus anchored to its lid, one of the tentacles poked into the slot as if it were fishing for letters.

The sun was beginning to set at the top of the valley as he pulled into the gravel driveway of a small inn. The chimneystack smouldered, greasy lights splashing the insides of the windows.

"This'll have to do," he muttered. There was a tint of disdain to his voice, but he had to admit to himself that he was quite pleased to have found the quaint little place. The reluctance was forced; for who, he couldn't have said. He thought briefly of Jamie.

Tilley turned off the engine and sat for a moment, looking up at the inn through the windscreen. Both hands on the wheel, he grimaced at the soreness in his stomach and tensed his shoulders, as if hoping to squeeze the knots out of them. When this didn't work he relaxed his body and took in the face of the building. The wall was plastered in sections, thick and crooked wooden beams forming a crude cobweb between fragment-like wedges of grey flint and white, smooth stone. The windows were square and dimpled, thin runnels of knotweed snaking into the frames and up toward the sagging, thatched roof. Flowerbeds around the edges of the building had grown over, thick bulging tangles of green bunching into strangling fingers, the brittle grey roots of sawn-down ornamental trees punching violently into the walls. Above a wide oak double-door, a square sign swung near-soundlessly in the soft wind. He couldn't read it from here, but it was streaked with oily dials of colour.

His eyes fell onto a wooden table beside the front door. An elderly couple sat on the attached benches, a pair of pint glasses and a couple of recently-cleared plates between them. The woman must have been eighty-odd, with thin white hair and the ridges of her shoulderblades pushing up through a sage-green cardigan like the stubs of sawn-off wings. She was hunched over her glass, fiddling with a pack of cards; it looked as though she were shuffling. The man across from her was bald, save for the tufts of grey above his large, almost bat-like ears. His eyes were wet and kindly. He was watching Tilley across the driveway. Locking eyes with the man, he nodded. Tilley nodded back. The man turned back to his card game.

Tilley swallowed nervously. He must have been a few years younger than the old pair, but he felt decidedly mortal watching them now. The symptoms of age were perhaps more apparent in their soft features, in the way they sat, but they looked happy. Almost youthful, in the way they snatched cards from each other and laughed. He glanced up into the rearview and his lips pressed tightly together. His skin was losing its healthy pallor, his eyes dulling a little every day. How much longer could he do this?

Not much longer, if the doctors have anything to say about it.

So why not pack it in? Why not retire and enjoy his last few years – months, perhaps, at this point – in peace? Again, he thought of Jamie. The time he could have spent with his son. With his wife. Why couldn't he at least spend the rest of his time with them?

"Because it's too late," he whispered, breaking eye contact with his reflection. He took a deep breath. It did him no good, this. Thinking about what could be. What could *have been*. His knuckles had gone bone-white, bulging against the skin. He let go of the wheel and massaged the bridge of his nose. "Oh, Christ… what's the fucking point?"

Tilley shoved open the driver's-side door and stepped out of the car, immediately enveloped by a blanket of cooling air. Purposefully he slammed the door and strode to the boot, forcing it open with the squeal of unoiled hinges. A flocked grey overcoat lay folded on top of the spare tyre; he reached for it and shrugged it on. Beside the tyre a thick, black briefcase was bolted shut, the digits on two combination padlocks scrambled. Nonetheless, the contents of the case seemed to pulse quietly through the leather, calling to him in ignorance of the locks…

Tilley closed the boot and stuffed his hands into his

pockets, heading across the gravel.

The old man looked up again as Tilley approached the front door, raising his pint glass. "Evening, sir," he said cheerfully. "Long drive?"

"Passing through on business," Tilley smiled politely. "Do I not look like a regular?"

"If you were, we'd know you!" said the old man's snap partner, reshuffling her cards without looking up. She giggled. "We know everyone round here."

"That we do, Mare," the man nodded, taking a drink before returning his glass to the table. "That we do."

Tilley paused at the front door, the sign swinging above him. "Anyone new round these parts?"

"Only yourself," the old woman said, turning her head to him. She smiled. She smelled faintly of petunias, Tilley noted.

"Fair enough."

"This is Mary," the elderly man said, nodding. "My wife."

"And yourself?"

"Johnny," he beamed.

"Huh," Tilley smiled back. "I'm a Jonathan myself. Jonathan Tilley. I go by Jack, though."

"That'll save some confusion," Mary giggled.

"Gotta know who's who round here," Johnny agreed seriously. "Go and grab yourself a drink, son. If you'd like to come sit with us, you feel free."

"Might be able to teach me how to shuffle these

fucking cards," Mary said, fumbling with a handful.

Tilley laughed, almost shocked by the curse-word. "You sure I won't find some more cultured company inside?"

"Oh, not tonight," Johnny said. "Quiet night."

"Well then, you just keep me a spot for later, all right?"

The old man threw him a mock salute. Tilley glanced up before opening the door to step inside, catching sight of the swaying wooden sign above his head. The wood was splintered, the paint vibrant despite some obvious wear: the artist had depicted, in gruesome accuracy, a trio of hounds pinning a squealing wild boar to the grass, the oily sunset behind the animals a bizarre window into the sky outside of the valley. The look of terror in the boar's eyes was dreadful, almost human. Beneath the painting were engraved the words *The Catch Dog*.

"Lovely," he whispered, and he pushed open the door.

The bar and restaurant were empty.

Tilley stepped out of the vestibule and crossed cautiously to a long, oak bar, marvelling at the wall decorations. The faint sounds of laughter from the old folks' table outside followed him in. A dozen or so round, mismatched tables stood on plush red carpet, bathed in the flickering light of a dim fire in a stone hearth to his right, encircled with a horseshoe of waist-high iron bars. Gritty, black-and-white photographs depicted hunting scenes all around him, framed in varnished wood with gold inlay and hung from the wattle-and-daub. Small trophies hung between the photos: behind him, a crest of stiff sika antlers; to the left, a selection of stuffed deer heads. A taxidermied fox stalked the mantelpiece, ears pinned back, eyes oily and unblinking.

Above the bar, between shelves of spirits and wax-dipped bottles of wine, hung an enormous stag skull, the eyes ragged downward caverns, the antlers sprawling and claw-like. The dome of the skull was cracked faintly, the whole of its pointed muzzle a decadently polished cream. It had been a real beast, when it was alive. Tilley coughed as he looked up into its hollow eyes, raising his wrist to his mouth. The cough was awful and wet and it buckled his stomach violently. When it was finished, he wiped his lips, checked his hand, and slid it back into his pocket.

"Help you with anything?"

Tilley turned, smiling weakly at the woman who'd appeared at the end of the bar. Her features were hard, but pleasant, and pinned quite curiously on him.

"Not to presume you're the landlady," Tilley said, "but I was hoping for a room."

"Just the one night?" the woman said, stepping

behind the bar and leaning down for something. She might have been in her mid-thirties, dressed in a crumpled lumberjack's shirt and jeans. Her dark hair was pulled into a messy bun behind her head. Before he could answer she produced a heavy, leather-bound ledger, dropping it heavily onto the bar. The clap echoed through the inn like the report of a pistol and she looked up sheepishly. "Sorry. Quiet night."

"So I've heard."

"Thirty pound a night," the landlady said, running her finger down the margin of the open page. "We've only got the one room up there, so I just need to check… it's free until Monday night. If you need any longer than that, there's a bed and breakfast the other end of town."

"No, that should be fine. I should be finished by then."

The landlady cocked an eyebrow and for a moment he wondered if he'd been too obnoxiously cryptic. The last thing he wanted was for her – or anyone – to start asking questions. Instead, she offered a hand across the bar. "Hayley. Hayley Manser."

"Tilley," he said, shaking her hand firmly.

"You've met my regulars, I take it," Hayley said, nodding toward the vestibule. Her eyes were a bright, sharp blue, her jaw perfectly curved. A curl of her hair – soft, almost feathery brown – had fallen into her face.

"Oh, Sid and Nancy out there? Yeah."

Hayley smiled. "Lovely couple. Listen, I'm going to check on them quickly before I go make up your room. You need a drink? Anything to eat?"

"Love a lager," Tilley said. "Something dark, if there is any."

"Coming up," Hayley said, moving down the bar to pick up a pint glass. "You okay with a single bed, by the way? I tend to move the double into my room when it's quiet, and I wasn't expecting anyone, but I can always swap them back—"

"No, no, single's fine," Tilley said. The landlady finished pouring, then sliced off the head of his pint and slid it across the bar to him. "How much?"

"I'll put a couple of quid on your bill for the night," Hayley smiled. "Anything else, you just let me know."

He nodded his thanks and drank. The lager was cool and perfectly spiced, and he settled onto a stool, pleasantly warm in the light of the fire across the inn. Hayley slipped out from behind the bar and crossed the restaurant, disappearing out of the vestibule. The door of the *Catch Dog* swung behind her.

Tilley was staring into the fire when he heard the faint trickles of subdued conversation behind him. Carefully, he put down his pint and tipped his head a little, turning his ear toward the still-swinging door. A wedge of orange sunlight swelled and narrowed in the frame, swelled and narrowed again.

"…asked about newcomers," he heard faintly, and

swallowed.

"You think this is about the girl in the old vicarage?"

"She's nabbed enough from the allotments on Dunnock Street"—this was Hayley—"I did wonder if Marge might call the police, you know."

"He's not police." Johnny. "No uniform, for one thing."

"D'you think he's—"

At this point the door finally clicked shut and the voices became too muffled to discern.

Tilley turned his face to the bar, once again looking up into the eyes of the monstrous stag skull. Long, hooked shadows spread behind the antlers, infecting every glass and bottle on the shelves either side of the hunting trophy with spangles of darkness. Tilley took another drink, cringing as his throat burned softly.

Tilley's room was surprisingly roomy, the single bed hammered against the wall beneath a tall, soot-stained window. The ceiling was high and the lamp hanging above the bed was an enormous, frosted bulb contained within an ornate iron sconce; it was turned off when he pulled his duffel bag over the threshold, and the walls were splashed with faint blue shadows. The sunset outside had mostly passed, leaving only the faintest pink traces among an otherwise-darkening bowl of deep purple sky.

Quickly he shut the door behind him and turned on the light, turning to admire a large pine wardrobe standing in the opposite corner. The wall to his right was all exposed brick, much of it trickling and spilling into thin wedges of mortar; a row of hooks had been suspended halfway up, screwed to a thick slab of driftwood. A chair and writing desk stood beneath them, an ovular mirror fastened to the back of the desk.

Tilley heaved his bag onto the bed and reached into his pocket for his mobile. Every operative of the British Witch Finders Agency was provided with a company phone, a slim touchscreen that was equipped with a sensitive tracking device, as well as a whole host of features Tilley didn't entirely trust. Elena had given up trying to contact him on the smartphone a long time ago; probably around the time he'd mailed it into the office in precisely-broken pieces. Flipping open his Nokia, an ancient thing he'd carried with him for years and one that he was confident was *not* monitoring his every move, he was momentarily dismayed to see that he had no service – moving to the window, however, the phone picked up a bar and the faint, pixelated trace of a second, and he froze in place to take advantage of them both.

Here, he typed with one bony thumb, his teeth firmly clamped together. He coughed into his elbow and hit *send*, directing the text message to Elena's assistant at the agency. He doubted she would alert Elena that he had arrived, but he had been told to let somebody know when he pulled up. He figured this would do.

There was a knock at the door, and Tilley slid the phone into his coat. "It's open," he called, turning his head.

The door opened and Hayley peered in, smiled across the room at him. "Happy with everything?"

"Perfect," he said. "Thank you."

"Anything else I can do for you?"

Tilley paused, ruminating. "Yeah," he said eventually, "what can you tell me about this place?"

"The inn?"

"The village."

Hayley shrugged. "It's quiet. You've probably gathered as much. It's always been quiet. Used to be farming land all around. Sheep, I think. Up on the hill? That's all gone now. miners came in the forties, blasted a bunch of rock out of the side of the valley, left again. A lot of the people who'd lived here at the time either left when the miners came, or left when they blew the hillside. Anyone who'd stayed through all that left when the miners did. That was Thatcher. You know how it goes. Town grows reliant on something, then it gets taken away… then all that's left are the houses."

"You'd think they would have been flattened."

"Protected," Hayley supplied matter-of-factly.

"Listed buildings, most of them. Just… sat empty for a while. Filled up again, eventually. Mostly in the nineties."

"What about before all that?"

"Before the miners?"

"Before the farmers."

"Hunting ground," Hayley said. "The forest spilled into the valley back then. No village, no people. Just a couple huts and a few foxes."

"And boar?" Tilley said, remembering the bar's sign.

"Oh yeah. Lots of boar."

Tilley smiled thinly. "Funny, isn't it? How things change."

"Things don't change, they get replaced," Hayley said. "The hunters were replaced with farmers, the farmers with miners… the miners with Thatcher, then with nothing."

"We'll call Thatcher an outlier."

"Call her worse, if you like," Hayley said with a raised eyebrow. "Then the nothing gets replaced with… well, *us lot*, I guess… you have to wonder what's coming next."

Tilley turned back to the window, looked vaguely outside. His teeth had clamped together again.

"Anyway, I'll let you get some sleep."

"I might go for a walk," he said quietly. "You lock that front door at night?"

"There's a key hanging in the wardrobe," the landlady said. "Come and go as you like."

"Thank you. Goodnight, Hayley."

"Goodnight yourself."

The door closed quietly behind her. After a moment the sconce above Tilley's head flickered softly. Somewhere distant, he heard the long, low bellow of a cow.

APRIL

April Leek had moved into the empty vicarage on Low Church Lane at the beginning of November, shortly after the death of her father on October 31st. The weather had remained high and pleasant, summery touches clinging to the trees as a delayed autumn pushed desperately to reach the end of its shift and let winter take over. The ice caps were melting, she supposed (she had recently heard, in fact, of an enormous shift in the water levels at the North Pole, though there had been rumours that was nothing to do with global warming), so why should she be surprised that the seasons were more temperamental these days?

After all, it was the least of her concerns.

Withdrawing a packet of cigarettes from her coat pocket, April tucked one between her teeth and fumbled for her keys. She looked around as she butted the door open, wary that somebody from the village might be watching her. They were mostly old folks, she knew, and had little concern for her, but she knew that some were suspicious types. Attention of any kind was the last thing she needed. This was why she walked two or three towns over when she needed food; to be caught swiping the odd vegetable from the allotments was one thing, but to be labelled a shoplifter in a town with only one general store and one (abandoned) petrol station was another entirely.

The entrance hall was long and narrow, snaking backward between the leaning, white-plaster walls to a thin staircase. On her left, beyond a coatrack and a small glass-fronted cabinet, were the doors to the kitchen-diner and lounge; on the right, a small storage cupboard beneath the stairs and two small windows – more like portholes, really – through which she could see the church and a few of the nearby terraces.

April moved swiftly to the kitchen, slipping off her shoes and padding in her socks across the uneven stone flags. She had been lucky to get such a good rental agreement, and had even persuaded the landlord to give her a couple months before he started pestering her for rent; this would give her enough time, she hoped, to find a decent part-time job (if nothing better came along). In the meantime she had promised to take good care of the old house, and the elderly landlord seemed satisfied. It would save him a few trips a month, she supposed. Looking for work had so far been difficult – she had just dropped out of college, for one thing – but her circumstances were not exactly unexceptional. She would find something.

She couldn't have stayed in that house. Not after what had happened there.

Not after Aunt Coral.

April stuffed a few things into the fridge, cringing as a wall of guilt rushed at her. Every item in there had been stolen, as had most of the cans in the cupboards. She had managed to bring a surprising amount of food and clothing with her, but only as much as she could carry onto the bus. She fumbled in the cutlery drawer for a lighter and ignited the cigarette between her lips, taking a long drag and closing her eyes. A plume of smoke blossomed before her face as she released it; another inward breath detonated the calming chemicals in her brain. Or she imagined it did, anyway. Her anxiety was running high. She resented smoking, but she hadn't touched a drop of alcohol since Halloween, and hoped not to for the foreseeable future; she knew that this was not an entirely preferrable vice, but it was the best she could do.

After counting slowly to ten in her head, she pulled

the frozen peas from her pocket and opened the freezer door. The freezer was separated into three compartments – two drawers and a pull-out shelf – and she quickly dumped the peas onto the shelf. The middle compartment was full. The bottom drawer…

She paused, staring down at the bottom drawer. Cold air billowed out softly, bathing her shins. The clear plastic was frosted and she couldn't see inside, but a dark, brown smudge pressed against it.

Slowly she bent down. Reached for the drawer's white plastic handle.

She had to see. Had to know that *it* was still there.

That it was still frozen.

Exhaling smoke, she gripped the handle and pulled out the drawer.

Inside was a silently screaming snake, a King Cobra with its neck frills fanned out to the size of a splayed hand. Its jaws were open, fangs presented like tiny white knives. Its eyes were yellow and glaring, even with a patina of frost over them.

The snake was folded in on itself, frozen stiff, every joint in its long, black body locked. It lay among shattered hunks of ice, mid-thrash, petrified like King Polydectes.

April slammed the drawer shut and stood up quickly – too quickly, making her brain jounce against the inside of her skull – then kneed shut the freezer door.

Emptying the rest of her pockets, April left the

kitchen and headed upstairs, stopping to pee quickly in the small bathroom at the top of the stairs before moving to her bedroom.

The snake's beady yellow eyes watched her through a film of frosty crystals as she moved, unable to shake the image from her mind. But it was still there, still locked away, frozen solid. It couldn't hurt her, not from in there.

She was safe.

Closing her bedroom door, she headed for the writing desk below the window and unlocked the drawer above the kneehole. Sliding it open, she laid a hand on the book inside. The cover was dark, wrinkled leather

(*like snakeskin*)

and the veins across its surface seeped with red. The pages were old and tattered. She closed the drawer and sat in her office chair, looking out onto the village. She could see the high street and the schoolyard, the inn the other side of town. A beaten Ford Focus pulled slowly down the street and turned into a cul-de-sac, headlights flaring quietly. Black Rope was starting to sleep.

For a few minutes she looked over the paperwork on her desk. The envelope had arrived that week, packed with a sheaf of documents and a stiff sheet of cardboard. They wanted her to sign off on her father's death before they released her inheritance. She supposed it was only fair.

Still, she hesitated.

When the cigarette had burned down to a stub, she poked it out in a small dish on the desk and reached for a pen. She twiddled this for a few minutes, reading the document in its entirety, then reading it again.

Aunt Coral had spoken of raising the dead. And April knew that these things, these impossible things, could be done – she had seen them happen, *made* them happen… she just had to find the right page. The right words.

Her eyes returned to the drawer above the kneehole.

Yellow eyes flashed inside her mind as she unlocked it again.

Jack Tilley stepped out of the front door and started across the Catch Dog's gravel driveway. Johnny had gone, he noted, but the old man's wife was still seated at the wooden dining table by the door. She turned toward him, her face bathed in moonlight, and smiled kindly. "Decided to come join us, then?"

Tilley paused. "Might have to take you up on that tomorrow, Mary. Sorry. Work to do tonight." He frowned. "Where'd your fella disappear off to?"

"Oh, Johnny's in the loo," the old woman said, nodding toward the inn. She giggled. "Still drinks like a dog after all these years. Started pissing like one too, now."

"You're a lot of fun, Mary," Tilley said, then he supplied a vague gesture and continued toward his car. "Take it easy, you two. I expect to see you both still at that table when I get back!"

Stone chips crunched under his boots as he marched to the Tasmin and unlocked it. He moved quickly to the passenger door, reaching inside to grab the sandwich bag off the seat. Inside the bag, the Hand of Michael twitched, bony knuckles grinding together as the fingers flexed, another small cloud of dust blooming off their sharp points.

Closing the door, Tilley returned to the car boot and heaved it open.

He had changed in the room, and now wore a smart, grey waistcoat and shirt beneath the overcoat. He had hoped to get moving earlier, but his medication had triggered a particularly unpleasant bout of coughing that had both delayed him and made a mess of his shirt. He felt bloated and indigested after his drink and there was an enormous pain in his breastbone. For ten minutes or so he hadn't been able to swallow and had thought, quite genuinely, that he might die then and there choking on the ball of saliva gathering in his throat.

Quickly he unlocked the briefcase. The two combination padlocks were to stop anybody from getting in; the bolt was to stop anything from getting *out*. He undid all three and flipped the lid.

Everything inside was arranged neatly in foam-walled compartments. An antique revolver lay in the corner of the briefcase, cushioned by soft padding and accompanied by six dull, unremarkable-looking bullets. A flask of holy water was fastened to the lid of the case, along with a selection of small, curved bones, each one engraved with arcane symbols and painted black. The witch finder's toolkit: a mix of curiosities and trinkets one might use to subdue an unholy target.

Tilley selected the undoing knife from its rectangular, foam compartment and sheathed it in his belt loops. The moon hung low above him in a star-speckled sky as he slammed the car boot and started back across the parking lot toward Black Rope's silent and only high street.

April stepped out into the night, taking a moment on the doorstep of the old vicarage to look up at the moon. It hung above the distant bulwark like a single great white eye, shining hungrily as the ragged stone mouth yawed open beneath. Behind her the pines rolled uphill, thick needled arms painted softly with grey, sharp points poking up into the stars. The trees heaved and swayed in a wind that carried down into the valley and fell quiet, swelling faintly.

She turned to lock the door, her hand trembling a little. She had been lucky to find the house, but it was deafeningly quiet inside and she needed a little fresh air. Most nights she found herself taking a walk round the village to clear her head, sometimes straying as far as the next town to check the noticeboards for job listings; she hadn't yet walked into the woods. April wasn't entirely sure her foraging skills were up to scratch, and didn't fancy heading into the dark – the forest was always dark, infinitely so, no matter the time of day – just to choke on a poisonous mushroom because she couldn't tell them apart. Were witches meant to be good at that kind of thing? She imagined so.

Am I a witch, then?

She supposed she must be, by definition. After all, what she had done to Aunt Coral…

Shuddering, she crossed the street and walked quietly in the shadow of the church. It towered over the vicarage, a looming tower thrusting up from ruined arches of flint and mortar. Great tree roots had been truncated around its base, some of them looping and twisting into the dull grey brickwork, many of them gnarled and snaggletoothed. The churchyard's low walls were overgrown with Berberis, spiky branches forming labyrinthine webs of tight thornwork; the sharp-edged plants had been planted around the perimeter to keep addicts out of the cemetery, but now they seemed vicious enough to discourage just about anyone. She had seldom seen anyone enter the churchyard, let alone the building itself. Strange, for a small town, but she imagined the building was just too ruined to pray in. Intact, mostly, save for the usual patches in the thatched roof and the cracks in the walls, but… haunted, somehow. As if something awful had happened here and the church had been allowed to fall into a special, dark kind of disrepair.

Leaving the church behind, April poked her headphones into her ears and stuffed her hands into her pockets, letting the music take her away. She walked down High Church Lane and the terraced houses thinned around her, the pavement on her left entirely crumbling into a green, tangled verge after a few minutes. Lights blinked on and off in the village, but she saw nobody else out on the street. Rope was an old town, and went to sleep early. She liked that.

Eventually she reached the end of the village and looped around the school building, her legs beginning to stiffen with the cold. Her breath bloomed in front of her face as a fine white cloud. Deciding to take a different route home, she wound her way into Rope Community Park.

Sparse lines of trees punctuated the winding dirt path through the sloping park, most of their branches bare. Wide swathes of lawn rolled and dipped either side of her, the old tennis courts on the left overgrown and unused; an ornamental fountain halfway along the path on the right was dry and smeared with white, powdery runoff streaks. Flowerbeds that might have been splashed with colour in the day were grey and muted palettes.

Cutting across the lawn, April found herself approaching a pair of wooden benches and, after a quick glance into the trees, perched herself in one of them and crossed her legs. She knew that it was only a ten-minute walk back to the vicarage, and wasn't ready to go back just yet. Hands still in her pockets, she looked out across the lawn and her eyes fell onto a section of the park that had been fenced off with brightly-painted iron railings. A kids' play area, complete with swings, a twisted metal slide that looked like an instrument of torture – she could almost feel the flesh of her back prickling with static and friction-heat as it dragged over the metal – and a seesaw composed of a thick iron wedge between two grinning carbon-fibre horses. Their mad white mouths flashed in the dark as the soft, swelling wind softly bobbed the seesaw.

A small silhouette sat on one of the swings, head bowed, hair falling in its face. The swing turned and twisted slowly as the silhouette kicked its legs, feet dangling a good twelve inches off the spongy tarmac beneath. April couldn't see the little girl's face, but the tiny dark silhouette was mousy and hunched, little hands firmly gripping the chains on either side.

Slowly April removed her headphones. The long,

low squeal of the chains whispered across the park toward her.

The little girl was alone. Nobody else out here but April, and now she felt oddly intrusive, as if she'd found herself looking in on the child's private routine. She turned her head away, looking into the trees at the path's edge. After a minute, though, she looked back toward the park. The girl's head was bobbing a little, as if she were crying.

April swallowed.

"Not your problem," she whispered, shoving her hands deeper into her pockets and looking away. *Don't draw attention to yourself. Don't talk to anyone you don't need to. Don't let them know your name.* She tapped her foot anxiously on the grass beneath her bench. "Not your problem. You don't need to get involved; not your problem, not your—"

The sound of a stifled sob found its way to her across the lawn.

"Fuck," April hissed, lurching up to her feet.

She walked calmly across the grass, the girl's silhouette clarifying as she drew nearer the iron railings. She must have been seven or eight, dark-skinned, with thick black hair matted to her cheeks. Tears ran slowly down her face as her chest shuddered quietly. She was wearing a fleece jumper that was much too large for her, her jeans scuffed and dirty. She looked up as April pushed open the iron gate with an awful wail. The girl's eyes snapped open wide, glittering white discs in the dark.

"Get away," she whispered. "I don't want to talk to you."

April raised both her hands, quickly shaking her head. "It's okay. You don't have to. Just… are you okay? I'll leave you alone if you tell me to. I just have to ask."

The girl said nothing. Her mouth opened, then closed again. She frowned.

"It's okay. You're not supposed to talk to strangers, I know that," April said. She swallowed, looking around the park. The shadows between the trees had thickened. Impossible to know if anyone was watching. "You don't have to talk. Nod or shake your head, all right? Are you okay?"

The girl hesitated. It seemed a full minute had passed before she shook her head.

April lowered her hands, still standing in the gateway. "You live round here?"

The girl blinked, then nodded. She sniffled, wiping her nose on the back of her hand.

"You locked out?"

The girl shook her head. Before April could come up with her next yes-or-no question, she spoke, her voice timid and quiet. "I don't want to go home."

"Why not?" April said, taking a step closer. When the girl flinched, she raised her hands again, just halfway up her chest this time. "What's at home?"

The child said nothing.

"Is it Mum and Dad?" April said. "Are they fighting?"

"How do you know that?" the girl said, frowning as she raised a hand to her mouth and gently poked her thumb between her teeth.

"It's what parents do," April smiled weakly. "I know how you feel, kid. Do you… do you come out here a lot?"

The girl nodded.

"What's your name? You don't have to tell me, if you don't want—"

"Nora."

"Nora. That's a nice name."

"I hate it."

"Well, that's fair enough," April said. "Listen, when Mum and Dad fight, is it… is it bad?"

Nora blinked again, the white discs in her eyes temporarily extinguished. "You mean do they hit each other."

"No, I… well, okay. Yes, I do. Do they?"

"I don't want to talk about it."

April felt a swell of anger in her chest. "Do you need me to go talk to them?"

Fear flashed across the girl's face.

"It's okay, it's okay… I'm not going to get you in trouble. Okay?" *Don't get involved. Don't get involved. Don't get involved.* "But if you need me to talk to them, or tell the police, or somebody else—"

The girl turned her head, looking across the park. April made a quick mental calculation and discerned that she was looking in the direction of the high street. "It's not that bad," the girl said quietly. "I don't think they mind being hit. They're not really fighting."

April swallowed, feeling vaguely sick. "Do you ever get hit?"

The girl looked at her again. "Not if I stay out of the way."

"I'm sorry," April said. "Listen, I live at the old vicarage. You know, on Low Church Lane? Nora, if you ever… if you want to come get out of the way somewhere a bit less cold, you just come knock on my door. Okay? I can leave you alone, you'll have the living room all to yourself, DVDs, books… you could freeze out here, if you're out too long."

Nora seemed to consider. Her hands were still tightly gripping the chains of the swing. There were faint bruises on her neck, April noted, starting to seethe again.

"Thank you," the girl said quietly.

"You just knock anytime. And if you need the police—"

Nora shook her head quickly.

"Okay. Well, you just stay safe, okay? You know where the vicarage is?"

"Yes."

"Don't get too cold, Nora."

"Okay."

April took a deep breath, briefly glanced toward the high street, then said, "Goodnight, Nora. Come see me anytime."

She turned and left the play area, the gate squeaking closed behind her. With one last look at the girl on the swings – Nora's head was lowered again, her black hair a thatch of shadow across her face – she crossed the park and headed home.

INTO THE VALLEY

Jack Tilley moved slowly down the high street, the Hand of Michael balanced on his upturned left palm. Still in its sandwich bag, the thing rustled gently as it pointed, flexing its index and middle fingers and jabbing their bony points vaguely in the direction of the old church. The way the Hand moved was almost spider-like, wriggling its fingers like chitinous legs, rolling its knuckles through the cracked nubs of dehydrated meat that held them together. It clicked and snapped whenever Tilley allowed his gaze to wander, demanding his focus. As he passed terraces and small shops with dark window displays, he followed the direction of the pointing fingers; when the Hand suggested he slip through a narrow alley between two narrow grey cottages, however, he continued forward. The thing would reroute him at the end of the street – Tilley just wanted to see a little more of the town before he found the witch's hideout. No doubt some local knowledge, however perfunctory, would come in useful.

The Undoing Knife seethed softly in the pocket of his overcoat.

The high street was wide, if dark, and though he walked in the glow of a row of street lamps many of them flickered, wedges of black scything through the cones of dim yellow they threw onto the tarmac. The pavement on his side was cracked, the kerb rising and falling in crumbling peaks and troughs; the other side was overgrown with weeds that slipped through old, damp picket fences. For a minute he gripped the hand and looked up toward the woods on his left, behind the church and a cluster of buildings that tipped up the slope of the valley. When he turned his gaze back to the street, he saw a trio of vague shapes coming along the road toward him. Dog walkers, a young-ish man and a woman in coats and scarves. It was getting chilly, he thought. It would soon be Christmas. Funny, he mused grimly, how every day seemed to last twice as long as the last, and yet the years shot by like throwing knives.

"Evening," he called, glancing down at the hand. It twitched, pointing to the houses on his left – *past* them – and he made a note to look out for another alleyway. Wouldn't do any good to have the last surviving piece of the Archangel Michael sulking at him for not following its directions.

"Evening," the woman called back. She was in her mid-thirties, brown hair swinging in a bob around a pretty face. Her scarf was a thick, layered clump of knitted colour around her throat. She held her husband's arm in one hand, the dog's lead in the other. "Are you looking for the pub?"

"Just came from there," Tilley smiled, tucking the Hand of Michael into his coat. "Lovely village."

"Isn't it?" said the dog-walker's husband, beaming.

As they passed him, Tilley glanced down at the dog, a golden-coated thing with dark ears and a squarish muzzle; it looked like a German Shepherd crossed with a greyhound. Powerful and muscular, grinning from ear to ear with its big, pink tongue hanging out. "Beautiful dog," he said. Smiling faintly: "Good night."

The couple and their dog slipped past him down the street and he retrieved the Hand from his pocket. With some anxiety it jabbed at the corners of the clear plastic bag, hooked fingers pointing to the left. Tilley looked along the terraces and saw a scraggly dirt path between two small front lawns. Ducking an overhanging knot of wisteria, he glanced back in the direction of the dog-walkers and watched them shrink, laughing, down the street.

Tilley headed down the path, pausing halfway along to cough in the shadow of the taller terrace. His throat constricted with pain and he clutched his chest, struggling for breath. After a minute, he continued.

He followed the Hand past the church and around the back of another row of terraces, seven or eight of them arranged in a crude semicircle. The smell of woodsmoke seeped past him and he noted a thin plume of grey rising from a crooked chimney stack. As he passed the third or fourth house, he heard the *nok! nok! nok!* of a butcher's knife on a chopping board and glanced into the low kitchen window to see a faint silhouette working at a countertop. The kitchen window was open and steam rolled quietly outside.

When he reached the vicarage, he stuffed the Hand of Michael into his pocket. It had confirmed his suspicions, at least.

Checking that the Undoing Knife was still in his coat – it was, and the blade was cool and angry – he looked vaguely up at the moon and steeled himself. Then, straightening his collar, he approached the house.

***

The book was ancient and heavy, weighing about as much as a breeze-block with thick, leathery pages and a cover as wrinkled as the surface of the moon. She heaved it out of the drawer and onto the desktop, suffocating the paperwork regarding her father's death

(*murder*)

underneath.

Drawing a deep breath, April brushed the pads of her fingers over the cover. Her bedroom was unlit but for the amber lamp on the corner of the desk and the speckled light of the moon filtering in through the window. Her cheeks were made soft by the faint glow, her eyes sharp and glinting. The cover of the book felt like snakeskin – she shuddered, the bright yellow eyes of the King Cobra folded up in the freezer flashing in her mind – smooth, rigid leather folded into hard veins, reddened with blood and scorched by fire. She was ninety per cent sure that the cover *was* skin, of some kind, but dreaded to think what reptile might have given it up to the witch who'd written the thing. Even worse was the knowledge that the pages, which were pinkish in places but had yellowed over the years, were probably a kind of stretched, treated skin too. She had no trouble imagining the poor animal whose back *that* had been ripped from.

April reached up to tie back her hair, closing her eyes for a moment. Somewhere outside an owl cawed from the direction of the forest. A dog barked sharply in response: the Steers, April thought; they always walked Chase around this time of night, and Paul Steer would walk the animal twice more during the day while Sharon was in the city.

She opened the book to the first page.

Her breath caught in her throat as her eyes tracked down the leather, and before she could stop herself from crying she was reading through a bleary lens. This was the page she'd opened that night, Halloween night, the page she'd read from when Aunt Coral had tried to kill her…

She turned away, looking out of the window. Long shadows crawled across the grass of a distant field. The open page screamed silently. Lines of Gothic black text ran like fleeing animals across creased yellow paper, the edges of certain letters outlined in red or gold or a bright, crystalline aqua; crimson decorations laced the borders and corners of the page and spilled between lines of calligraphy like runnels of blood. In the lower-right corner, a painting of an impish figure with a wide, toothy mouth screamed as his chest was shot through with a streaming orange light, depicted with bars of paint. The text was written in Latin – for the first few pages, at least – and she had at least been able to translate some of the earlier spells. A few pages in the language switched to something that looked like a crude form of Hebrew, then it became a complex code that seemed to use Ancient Greek as a base; she had decided that either the book had been written by multiple people, decades or even centuries apart – not to mention entire continents – or that whoever had written it had been a real arse. But then, if *she* had written a bunch of spells that could turn people

(*hunch miser in parvae agnitudinis creaturam convertam*)

into snakes, she would want to make them as difficult to decode as possible.

Wiping her eyes, she turned to the next page. The spread was punctuated with a number of intricate, spiralling patterns in red and yellow, and between the lines of black ink she had written a number of loose translations. Turning a few more pages, she came to a full spread depicting a hellish scene: rudimentary demons danced along the bottom of the page, a titanic creature that looked like an owl with great white flaring discs for eyes spreading its wings into the fiery ceiling above.

A tear fell onto the page and flattened on the owl's left eye. "Oh God," April whispered, turning her face again. The field outside was black and shimmering. "What the hell am I doing? What… what am I doing here?"

Aunt Coral had come at Halloween.

She was an oddly tall woman with a dome-shaped tumour between her shoulders; dressed in a black cape and a wide-brimmed plague doctor's hat, she had arrived a couple days before the big night – the night, Coral had told April, when the veil between worlds was thinnest. Coral had lost people, she explained that fateful night in the attic. Lots of people. And with the right magic, the right sacrifice, she would bring them back.

She had sacrificed April Leek's father two days before Halloween.

Coral had kept his body in a bag in the attic, chopped into pieces. April hadn't even known; had suspected, perhaps, that something was wrong, but only because Aunt Coral was the kind of person who made you feel that *everything* was wrong. Coral had used some strange magic to impersonate April's father on the phone, telling her that he was stuck out of town, that she'd have to look after her auntie for a couple days.

On Halloween Night, Coral had dragged her into the attic.

"Don't think about it," April whispered, turning the page again. "Stop thinking about it…"

One living sacrifice, and one already dead. That was what Coral had told her, in front of the swirling pool of mist she had raised from the attic floor. She needed April's blood, and her father's head. And for a moment April had been helpless, terrified, more bewildered than she had been in her life—

Then the book. She had grabbed it from the old

writing desk in the attic, fumbled for the first page

(*just like a college textbook*)

and screamed words she didn't understand into the miasmic vortex of the rafters, the wind of the underworld blowing about her face, until

(*the easiest spells are at the beginning*)

a gust of bloody power surged past her, surged through her, and then—

The book had slammed shut in her hands. Aunt Coral was gone. And in her place…

In her place, a snarling King Cobra. She had turned the old witch into a snake.

The spells she had translated so far had been similarly primitive – levitation, for one, was something she'd enjoyed practicing – and she had a feeling that what she was looking for would be somewhere near the back of the book, if it was in there at all. It had to be.

And she wouldn't sign those papers until she was sure there was no way to reverse it. To bring him back. To make things right. Anger flashed in her chest and she grimaced, a sick taste briefly resting in her mouth. Blinking away the last of her tears, April turned the page again. Another spread of black text, the letters completely unrecognisable – perhaps there was some way of correlating it to the earlier pages, or later ones even. Perhaps if she turned the book upside-down, laid certain pages over each other, tore the damn thing open…

"Useless," April snapped, slamming the book closed. She stood, frustrated, running her hands through her hair. Grabbed her hoodie off the back of the desk chair and slung it on, suddenly cold. There had to be something in there, something to fix all this. Aunt Coral was frozen, folded into leather coils, downstairs. But if what Coral had *done* could be *undone*—

Her train of thought was interrupted by a sudden knock at the front door.

April froze, temporarily confused. She leaned down to unlock her mobile phone – resting on the bedside cabinet the landlord had sold her – and checked the time. A little after nine. Not stupendously late, but late enough to make her suspicious. Then she remembered. The kid from the park, it had to be.

"Shit," she whispered. Hurrying out of the room, she called, "I'm coming, Nora, hang on!"

April tumbled into the entrance hall and practically fell into the front door, already thinking of all the hell she'd raise if the poor kid's parents had done anything to her. Quickly she twisted the knob and pulled the door open.

"Nora, come in, it's… oh. I'm sorry, who are you?"

She blinked at the old, bald man on the doorstep, quickly taking in the white streaks of scar tissue splashed across his face and the knife in his hand. Moving to slam the door shut, she was surprised at the speed at which the man jammed his foot into the crack.

"Nice to meet you," Jack Tilley said, smiling thinly in the moonlight.

55

UNDOING

Tilley stormed into the entrance hall, barrelling forward as April staggered away from him.

"Please!" she yelled, crying out as her ankle slammed into the bottom step and she steadied herself on the banister rail. "Get out! What do you—"

Tilley growled, grabbing the girl by the lapel of her hoodie and swinging her into the wall. She was younger than he'd expected – couldn't have been twenty years old, though she might have been approaching it – and lighter, too, and despite his age he was able to lift her off the floor as he slammed her back into the plaster. "Where's the book?" he snarled, brandishing the knife. The handle was a curved husk of polished ivory, the shape and size of the bone unpleasantly familiar; crude black runes had been carved into the hilt of the dagger and the blade was engraved with more of the same, these ones glowing faintly in the steel.

"I don't know what you're talking about," April choked, kicking out as she tried to bat Tilley's gnarled, bony hand away from her throat. Her head pounded. "Who the hell… are you?"

"Tell me where it is!" Tilley yelled, tightening his grip on the rib-bone handle of the Undoing Knife. Out of the corner of his eye he twigged a small leather pouch on the floor behind the open front door, about the size of a closed fist; a line of fine red power had been poured across the doormat. The heel of a boot – his boot – had scuffed the line near the middle, but it was otherwise intact. He recognised the powder and frowned. Turning back to the girl, he gripped the shelf of her jaw and shunted her another inch up the wall. "Where's the fucking book?"

April gasped, her throat and cheeks reddening. "I don't know any book—"

"Liar!"

"Leave me alone! I don't have a book, I don't know any—"

"*Liar!*"

Tilley yowled as April slammed a knee up into his

groin, a bolt of pain spreading quickly through his stomach. His grip on her neck loosened and she dropped to the floor, ducking under his fist as he swung it blindly. A well-placed fist connected with his ribs and he stumbled backward, his coat blowing open. The sandwich bag containing the Hand of Michael tumbled from his inside pocket, practically throwing itself to the floor in a frenzy of wriggling fingers. For a moment April was distracted, staring in awe at the convulsing severed hand stretching the corners of the clear plastic bag taut on the stone flags of her hallway floor. Tilley took advantage of the moment and barrelled into her, knocking her into the wall again. He turned away before she could fight back, scrambling for the Hand, and saw that it was pointing frantically upward with a jabbing, grey finger.

Upstairs.

"Get out of my house!" the girl yelled, slamming an elbow into his back. She certainly wasn't behaving like a witch. He had faltered, seeing how young she was – an experienced witch would have taken advantage of the moment of weakness and destroyed him by now. Tilley had seldom encountered a witch who'd rather throw her knee into his crotch than separate his head from his body. Especially one in possession of a book as powerful as the one Michael was agitatedly telling him was upstairs right now. This – trading physical blows with a teenager – was new.

Must be about time to retire.

Coughing, he stumbled onto the staircase, noting a trio of leather pouches like the one by the front door hanging from the banisters. A flash of unease pulsed in his brain – there was something wrong here, something to do with the bags—

"Get the fuck out of my house!" April screamed, and Tilley was flung into the banister rail. He buckled as the railing smashed into his side, wheeling around in the air to see the girl standing a dozen feet away, still in the hall, both her hands raised. The fingers were splayed wide, her arms trembling with power. The force of the spell had blown her back a little too – so she was powerful, he thought, but inexperienced – and it took her a second to draw her hands into an arc and send him crashing down onto the steps. Tilley yelled as his tailbone punched up into his ribs. Groaning, he grabbed for the rails and tried to heave himself up.

Down in the hall, April had doubled over, her chest heaving with the effort.

"You don't know anything about a book, huh?" Tilley wheezed.

"I might've picked up a few of the basics," April said, equally out of breath. "But I need it, you're not having it! Whoever the fuck you are"—she stood, thrusting out her hands and flexing the fingers, preparing to throw him again—"you better leave right now or I'll break your fucking legs!"

Tilley scrambled to his feet as the Hand of Michael thrust its fingers out of the sandwich bag, ripping four holes in the clear plastic with a sound like something damp stretching and snapping hard. The fingers curled tightly around April's ankle and twisted. She yelled, looking down and stamping her foot. Taking his chance, Tilley bolted up the stairs away from her.

"Hey! You get this fucking thing off me!" she called after him. Tilley cringed as he heard a sick, dry *crunch* and the dull scuff of the girl wiping her heel on the flags. That was another relic gone. A good one, too. Elena would kill him for that. "You stay out of there, you fucking psycho!"

"Sorry, Michael," Tilley whispered, pealing down the landing. With no Hand to point him in the right direction, he was forced to guess; he went for the door at the end of the hall that was slightly ajar. On the carpet at the foot of each door – three of them, narrow oak things set into worn frames – was another line of red powder and a small leather bag. It was witchcraft, certainly, but the kind that he wasn't used to seeing. *No, you* are *used to seeing it*, he thought, *but not as much as this. Not by witches.*

It was the kind of witchcraft that the Agency used. That the Agency 'borrowed,' he corrected himself, knowing that Elena would do the same if she was here. The kind that he wouldn't expect the owner of the book to deem necessary, not with the gruesome arsenal they had in their possession. The kind that witches only usually used as an afterthought:

Protection magic.

Protection, specifically, against other witches.

She's learned the basics, all right. And she was using them to… keep herself safe?

Tilley stormed into the girl's bedroom and saw the book splayed open on a writing desk by the window. Behind him he heard thudding footsteps coming up the stairs. He thought quickly: she was inexperienced, and he might be able to dispatch her quickly, getting her out of the way before taking care of the book; but the book was priority, and if the girl was able to stop him – after all, she might only have had the capacity for a little weak levitation magic, but she could land a mean punch – then he would fail altogether.

The book, then.

He tumbled across the room and steadied himself over the desk, brandishing the Undoing Knife and raising it high above his head. He felt a chill rush into the room behind him as the door swung open, the girl coming after him in a storm of rage and power. *"No!"* she yelled.

Tilley grunted as a wall of ice-cold wind smashed into his back, ploughing his already-bruised stomach into the desk. A thick, wet cough was forced from his lungs and a thin spray of blood danced across the corner of the book's open page. The knife tumbled from his hand and skittered over the table. He turned, already reaching into his trouser pocket. April glared at him from the doorway, both her hands raised, a thin dribble of yellow saliva running out of her mouth and trickling down her chin. Her eyes were wide, the irises clouded over so that only tiny black pupils remained. She was grimacing, witchcraft churning painfully throughout her body.

"You can't hold it!" Tilley yelled over the swirling wind. A cascade of cold air punched its way through the room, bouncing off every wall. He was pinned to the desk, unable to move. Struggling, he reached into his pocket and closed his fist around a thick, round wedge of brass: an ancient, scratched coin, bristling and hot with energy. He had more relics and devices on his person, many of them throbbing excitedly; another, hanging around his neck on a strong silver chain, pulsed quietly, and it was a struggle to resist the urge to use it – he shouldn't keep the damn thing so close, he knew that, it was too tempting—

Ripping the coin from his pocket, Tilley yelled into the wind and brandished it before his face. *"Air ais a steach ort!"*

A blast of heat launched itself from his palm, curling easily around the coin and blossoming to a shunting, invisible force that swelled into the room. April gasped as the wind funnelling into every corner of the room was sucked back toward her body, blowing her into the wall. There was a sickening *crack* as her skull bounced off the plaster, then she slid down to the floor. Turning desperately, Tilley scrambled across the desk for the Undoing Knife and grabbed it by the curved bone hilt.

"No!" April yelled, but before she could heave herself Tilley had slammed the point of the blade into the open pages.

"*Poništi ja štetata,*" he yelled, forming a crude imitation of Macedonian with his tongue, the words exploding out of his throat like bile. The knife sunk easily into the book, scything through leathery paper with a seething whisper. The pages fluttered around the blade as the runes etched into the steel flared white. "*Poništi smrt!*"

A thick, bulging knot of blood surged out of the book and flooded the surface of the blade, dampening the glowing runes as it filled them in and splashed the handle and Tilley's forearm. "What have you done?" April yelled as he wrenched the blade out of the book. She stumbled to her feet, locking both arms in front of her chest and forming a hooked ball with her hands. Thin wisps of black fog swirled around her wrists, spreading, thickening. "What the hell have you done?"

"This is the Undoing Knife!" Tilley yelled back, brandishing the thing. Blood oozed down the blade and hung in thick ropes from his fist. "Every spell you've cast using this book, I've reversed it! Everyone you've hurt—"

The black fog stopped swirling as April faltered. The colour returned to her eyes and she blinked. Her face was suddenly pale. "You've done *what*?" she whispered.

"The only thing I need to do before I destroy the book for good," Tilley growled. "Now—"

There was an awful *crack* from downstairs, the sound of something hard bursting open, then an awful shattering as something spilled across the flags in the kitchen.

"Wait," April said, her face flooded with horror, "that means…"

Beneath them there was a hard, echoing slam as the freezer door smashed into the worktops, then that dreadful wrenching plastic-breaking-apart sound as something forced its way out. An inhuman screech came to them from the kitchen and April moaned. Her attention was no longer on Tilley, but the open bedroom door and the landing beyond.

"Coral," she whispered.

CORAL

April tore out onto the landing before Tilley could stop her, pelting around the top of the banister rail and thundering downstairs.

"Stop!" Tilley yelled, keening across the room. He froze in the doorway, looking back over his shoulder at the ancient book on the girl's writing desk. The girl didn't matter, he knew that; it was the book, the book was what was important, the girl could wait—

He heard April scream downstairs and swore, staggering out of the room after her. He smelled sulphur as he reached the stairs, strong walls of the awful, sour stony smell pulsing up toward him, almost potent enough to knock him out. With the smell came an undercurrent of smoke and he feared for a moment that the house was on fire. Tearing down the last few stairs, he stumbled around the kitchen door.

The fridge-freezer had been blown back against the wall, the freezer door wide open. The drawers had shattered on the tiles, shards of clear plastic scattered across the floor among tiny pools of thawing frost. Bags of food had split open, a kaleidoscope of frozen peas and icy chunks of mince thrown into disarray around the edges of the room. The freezer itself was empty, a colossal dent bulging out of its side where something inside had exploded outward. April cowered in one corner of the kitchen, looking desperately around as if she'd just seen a wild animal. Her hands were splayed against the wall, hair in her face. She locked eyes with him for a fraction of a second and he saw real terror in them, genuine, unfiltered terror.

"What have you done?" she whispered. Then her eyes widened – she was looking behind him now, over his shoulder – and Tilley turned, staggering backward into the kitchen—

The crone had appeared behind him silently, impossibly. She was tall, despite the tumorous hump between her shoulders that thrust her neck and head forward; she towered over Tilley, a good six-six and as wide as a bear, her enormous bulk filling the entire doorframe. Her spine was curved, pressing against the folds of a web-like black cloak that tightly swaddled her whole body. She wore a wide plague-doctor's hat, the brim a discus of the same webby black lace and clearly decaying, the bowl pocked with tiny holes. Her eyes were tiny yellow points in a wrinkled face, her nose a great bird's beak, her chin jutting out from beneath a crooked, thin-lipped smile. The titanic woman was half-frozen, her cloak stiff and shiny and sprayed with moss-like patches of frosty blue crystal. Runnels of glittering ice poured down her chin and out of her nostrils, streams of fluid frozen and white; her flesh was pale and bluish.

"Shit," Tilley whispered.

A black-gloved hand appeared from within the witch's cloak, the hooked fingers spreading wide. The hand was more like a talon – Tilley couldn't help but compare the creature to a vulture or a buzzard – and the fingers were stiff, knuckles cracking audibly as flakes of frost shuddered off the claws and punctuated the air around her.

"Coral," April said behind him, "please, I didn't mean to, please… what's she doing? What are you doing?!"

The witch glared at Tilley, ignoring the girl, and grinned, twisting her talons into an eldritch sign. A second hand joined the first, thrusting out of the cloak and pinching at some invisible point in the air directly in front of her face, then the claws bent in on themselves, flexed outward, two fingers pointing up at the ceiling. Tilley's eyes widened as he realised what she was doing. He lurched forward, scrambling in his pocket for something to use, hoping that at least his body weight slamming into her stomach would give them a moment's respite even if he couldn't find anything—

A wall of sulphurous air slammed into his body and he was thrown backward, his rump hitting the stone tiles before his back smashed into the wooden counter behind him. He yelled, falling limp against the cupboard, went to struggle to his feet as the witch in the doorway continued her sign, clapping her wrists together before grabbing a handful of air and wrenching it counter-clockwise.

"No!" Tilley screamed.

Too late.

The kitchen filled with a flare of bright amber light, so silky and thick that it felt like an explosion, and he heard the witch laughing. She cackled loudly, her face appearing through a smog of orange mist as the flare dissipated. Tilley felt his heart sink into his stomach, horror and disappointment flooding his veins. He should have stopped her, should have been faster, but damn it, he was getting too old…

Behind him April blinked, her eyes adjusting to the light. The air hissed around them, stinking of bad eggs.

"What did she do?" she whispered.

Tilley swallowed.

Before he could answer, Coral stepped into the kitchen and spread her claw-like hands wide.

SUMMONING

The witch swept forward, her cloak billowing behind her and exposing bony hips and legs, putrid grey skin riddled with sores and boils. With her hands spread she formed two signs in the air then clapped her wrists together. "Cover your face!" Tilley yelled, but he was too slow to shield his own; a pulse of blood-red obliterated every particle of his vision as he raised his arm, and then everything went black.

"I can't see!" April screamed. "What the hell did she do?"

Tilley had no time to answer. He felt a presence materialise above him and lashed out blindly, slamming his elbow into the witch's decaying thigh. She didn't budge an inch and he yowled in agony as the tip of a single clawed, bony finger brushed his face, sending bolts of white-hot pain into his brain. The blinding spell was only temporary – he could feel it fading already – he just had to avoid her for long enough to regain his vision without her taking his head off.   She wasn't at full strength, he knew that; the blindness would have lasted for minutes if she was, and not seconds.

He felt her hand swinging toward him again and ducked his head, just in time. Her claws raked the air inches above his bald head.

Across the kitchen April pressed her back to the wall, hyperventilating. She knew that her eyes were open wide, knew that she hadn't somehow squeezed them shut in all the fear; the blackness that had fallen over everything was unnatural, not the blackness of the backs of her eyelids or even an extinguished lightbulb – this was a blanket of pure shadow, one that covered everything around her more than it covered her eyes. She began to blink frantically, swinging her head left and right as the shapes of the counters and cupboards started to clarify, the shadows draped over them thinning slowly – too slowly – she heard a dull *crunch* and Tilley screamed. Before she could yell out a massive dark shape flew through the blackness toward her, its edges barely discernible. She sidestepped as the great bird-like thing swiped at her with both hands, only just managing to avoid its talons.

"Get out of here!" Tilley yelled.

The blackness was fading now, but she had lost Coral, her head was moving too fast, all the dark shapes blurring together. "I can't!" she shouted. "I don't know where—"

A set of claws shot out of the darkness, inches from her face, raking at her eyes in four stripes of glaring, searing white. She keened back and her head smacked the wall. Colour was beginning to return, blooming in the corners of her vision, and she glimpsed Tilley crawling over the tiles, bringing something out of his coat. Then Coral's claws clamped themselves around her throat and she gasped, lifted off the floor, her legs dangling beneath her. Coral thrust her up toward the ceiling, incredibly strong, hissing all the while. Her eyes burned yellow in the dark, smouldering, thin cloudy trails of fire peeling from their corners.

April spread the fingers of her right hand wide and locked the knuckles of her middle and ring finger, pressing the pads to her palm. A knot of energy exploded from her chest and down the length of her arm, twisting her wrist as it left her body. Coral's grip loosened and she stumbled back a step, the yellow glare in her eyes momentarily flickering.

April fell onto her knees, gasping for air. "Ha!" she yelled, the kitchen swimming back into view. Behind the witch Tilley had scrambled to his feet and she looked up as he withdrew a slim silver cross from his coat, glancing at her frantically before ramming it into Coral's spine.

The witch hissed, turning on the old man lightning-quick. Her cloak was a thunderstorm of energy around her body, crackling with electricity as it blew into the kitchen. April lurched to her feet, panting, as Coral slammed the heel of her claw-like hand into the shelf of Tilley's chin and knocked him stumbling into the countertop.

April's eyes fell onto the cross lodged in Coral's back and she lunged for it, grabbing the thing with her right hand as she formed another sign with her left. The silver softly burned her palm and she yelped. Remembering the old man's knife, she quickly understood that the cross must have some kind of anti-witch dressing – or maybe it was the silver – and she grabbed it hard and twisted, hoping it was affecting Aunt Coral more violently than her. Coral screeched and April wrenched the cross free of her back before she could turn around, a wing of black blood spraying her legs.

Coral leered in her face, her maw opening wide beneath that beak-like nose, sulphur and fire pouring out. Coral's eyes were ablaze, yellow heat exploding from them and turning to grease in the air. April abandoned the spell she'd been conjuring with her left hand and slammed the cross into Coral's throat with the right. "Take that, motherfu—"

Coral's head shot back as the point of the cross burrowed into the roof of her mouth, thick trails of gelatinous yellow dribble running out of her lips. She staggered backward, grabbing at her neck, but April lurched forward with her, pushing it deeper, screaming into the woman's face. Coral's eyes flickered.

"Get back!" Tilley yelled. April released the cross, stumbling backward.

A fraction of a second later, Coral exploded.

Her hands spread wide, her shadow on the wall behind her forming the long, winged shape of a titanic vulture, then her body collapsed in on itself, a vortex of blood and bone forming as a ball of swirling red slop in the middle of her stomach before sucking all the flesh and cloth and hair inside itself; then it burst in a spray of black smoke and soot and disappeared. The kitchen lights flickered.

April fell down the wall onto her rump, panting hard.

Across the room from her Tilley clutched his chest, his face pale. He looked at her. "You all right, kid?"

April cocked an eyebrow, turning her face to him. "No!" she said, bewildered. "What the fuck, man?"

Tilley stumbled, coughing into his arm. Once the cough had begun it wracked his throat for a full minute, wet and awful. April watched him buckle over, then fall to his knees.

"What the hell is going on?" she asked quietly, when another minute had passed.

"I need to know… who she was," Tilley said. "What she was. Why she was here."

April swallowed. "She was my aunt Coral. She was a witch. She… tried to kill me, a little while ago. Halloween. She needed me and my dad for a spell."

Tilley looked at her. "Your dad?"

"Yeah. He… he didn't make it."

"I'm sorry," Tilley shook his head, still trying to catch his breath. Around them particles of bloody soot floated quietly in the air, the remnants of Aunt Coral smouldering almost calmly. "What about you?"

"I stole her book," April said. "Turned her into a snake."

Tilley smiled thinly. "Then you put her in the freezer."

"Yeah. I didn't know what else to do."

"Okay," Tilley nodded.

"I didn't know she'd turn back into… her."

Tilley closed his eyes, pressing his head back against the counter. "She shouldn't have," he said. "It's my fault. The Undoing Knife. I… I was sent here to destroy the book you stole. The Knife is a relic, there are a few of them in the Agency's possession. It… it reverses any spell cast by the book's current owner. That's you."

April stared at him.

"I didn't know," he shook his head. "The book is evil, kid. You know that. I wasn't to know you might have used it to—"

"Are you shitting me?" April snapped. "You didn't think to ask me? You just stormed in here and fucking—"

"I followed procedure," Tilley said calmly. "If you'd killed her, this wouldn't have happened."

"Oh, fuck off. You ever killed a family member before?"

"Yes."

April froze. "I'm sorry, what?"

Tilley shook his head again. "Not now. Look, I'm sorry. But the book still needs to be destroyed."

April looked at him for a long time, seething. Then she said, "She's gone, right? It's over?"

"She's gone," Tilley said.

"Good. Okay. Well, then, the book—"

"But it's not over."

April blinked. "What?"

"Before she cast the blinding spell," Tilley said, "she made a summoning."

"A what?"

Tilley closed his eyes. His chest heaved a little. The smell of sulphur had not begun to fade, and April's throat was clogged with it. "There's a hierarchy," Tilley said. "Witches… there are covens, and there are overseeing bodies. When an experienced witch is in danger, she might alert others – superiors – to her location. Summon them."

"Why?"

Tilley shrugged. "Vengeance. Retribution. Justice."

"So who did she summon?" April whispered.

Tilley's eyes snapped open. He looked darkly at her. "If we're lucky, somebody from her coven. Another witch. That won't be too difficult to deal with, as long as they don't summon anybody else."

"And if we're unlucky?"

"The Parliament," Tilley said.

A beat. "When will we know—"

The kitchen shuddered softly. It wasn't a rumble, more of a vibration, and it only lasted a second. But they both felt it.

"Soon," Tilley said.

Hayley Manser was wiping glasses behind the bar when her chest exploded, a thick spear of ice punching into her heart. Her lungs exploded through her ribs – or felt as though they had – waves of hellfire pouring through her insides. The glass fell from her hand but she didn't hear it shatter between her feet; her head keened back, the bones and cartilage in her throat cracking audibly as a pillar of blackness drilled up into her skull. She tried to scream but couldn't; the pain was too great. Eyes open wide she shrieked silently at the ceiling, the titanic stag skull grinning cruelly on the wall behind her.

Her hands spread and a piercing yellow light detonated in her eyes. For a full minute they burned, greasy streamers of gold pouring up into the air from inside her skull. Then she took a staggering step backward, blinked, and the light was gone.

She stood still for a moment. Then, as if waking from a bad dream, she reached up and cracked her neck. "Oooh…" she whispered. Her voice was different. Inhuman.

Flexing her knuckles with a bony crunch, she leaned forward and dug her fingers into the bar. Drool ran in a thick, gluey string from her mouth, running slowly down her chin and neck. Absent-mindedly she wiped it away.

Her eyes flickered yellow.

Halfway down the high street, a little over half a mile from the Catch Dog, moonlight glinted cruelly in the silver discs of a powerful Alsatian-greyhound cross's eyes.

Anna tightened her grip on the dog's lead as his spine buckled, his haunches raising so hard she heard the animal's shoulders cracking. "Lieutenant Dan!" she hissed, recoiling. The dog's muscular shoulders rolled, his head snapping left and right. His movements were erratic and distressing, his haunches rising and falling as if he were trying to vomit, his spine twisting, wrenching his hips in violent circles. The lead went taut and Lieutenant Dan reared his head, snout yawing open as a dreadful, guttural moan escaped his throat. "Lieutenant – Danny, Danny, stop it – stop it, please—"

The dog ignored her, shaking his head, ears twitching madly as though batting at flies. The animal's whole body was bucking and convulsing now, the audible crunch of bone on bone rippling through the stiff night air. Lieutenant Dan's muzzle dropped suddenly and viscous, yellow strings of drool swung from his lips.

"Danny," Anna said, tugging on the lead, "what is it? Get up, please – help me, Gary, for Christ's sake, help—"

The dog turned his head and grinned back at her. Anna had to stifle a scream.

Lieutenant Dan's face had changed. The kind, always-smiling face of the dog they had adopted from the rescue centre out in Whisford had sloughed back, ripped apart by the snarling muzzle of a wild animal. His black lips were peeled back from rows of teeth which suddenly appeared sharper, smashed together in knobbly purple gums. His eyes flickered a hellish mustard-yellow, narrowed to points in sockets that looked like tight black holes.

"Gary," Anna whispered, turning her head, "please…"

Gary looked blankly at her from the pavement. Anna's husband stood still, his hands hanging limply by his sides, his tall figure slanted slightly – one shoulder dipped beneath the other, one knee slightly buckled, as if he hadn't quite learned how to stand.

His face was the same as Danny's. His smile was thin and cruel, his eyes vacant and tinted with that awful, flickering yellow film.

Anna swallowed. "Oh God," she whispered, "oh, what the hell is—"

Her head tipped back suddenly, a bolt of pain rocketing up her neck. Before she could scream she felt something slip into her chest and spread, faster than fire, an inexplicable presence, a thick and strangling darkness that was cold and hot and inevitable. She opened her mouth and her jaws cracked open, her body struggling to keep itself together with the flood of smoke and soot through her veins. Her ribcage cracked loudly, her spine twisting into knots. Her fingers splayed outward; the lead fell from her hand as her elbows bent back. Her eyes flared a brilliant, burning yellow, then the colour faded to that dim lamplight glow that sparkled in Lieutenant Dan's face and her husband's. Her entire body was wracked with pain, her mind exploding from some fathomless centre into a vortex of absolute nothingness.

Anna's chin dropped to her chest. She swayed on her feet for a moment, then bolted upright again.

She looked at Gary and smiled, her eyes flickering yellow. Slowly she bent down to pick up Danny's lead. The dog snarled, but did not attack.

A moment passed, then the three of them started to walk down the high street toward the old vicarage.

Outside the bar, the elderly couple sat either side of their permanently-reserved picnic bench, chins pressed to their chests, a pack of cards scattered on the wood between them. A pint glass had toppled and produced a small pool of softly-crackling foam on the gravel beneath. Anyone walking by might have assumed the old pair were sleeping.

Slowly, Mary raised her head. The bones in her neck popped loudly, one by one. She smiled. "Oh, this one's out past her bedtime," she whispered, her voice thin and shadowy. Her eyes flickered faintly. "I might have to swap her for something a little stronger."

Across the bench from her, Johnny tipped his head back, his own eyes still blaring yellow. His body heaved, shuddered, and stilled. He opened his mouth wide, as if testing the jaws. The glow of his eyes began to diminish.

"How's yours?" Mary asked.

"Weak," he shrugged, tilting his head left and right. "Old. A little drunk."

"Shame. You deserve better."

"He'll do for now," smiled the thing in Johnny's body. "And if he breaks, I'll find another."

The girl writhed and bucked in the swing-seat, gripping the chains with her tiny hands. Her knuckles were bone white, her face pale in the moonlight. Her head was wrenched back from her shoulders with a mighty *crack* and she yowled in pain, screaming jets of mustard-yellow light punching out of her eye-sockets and into the dark. Nora's chest sunk into itself and her legs kicked, out of control; her fingers split open and she tipped over backward, losing her balance and toppling off the swing.

For half a second, she floated: an inch off the damp bark beneath the swing, the girl hung suspended in the air. Her eyes were wide open, yellow fire crashing out of them, thin wisps of it flowing out of her mouth and nostrils. She fell, hitting the ground softly, her eyes snapping closed.

She convulsed for a while, then the fits started to slow. Eventually, Nora rolled onto her back.

One eye was yellow and flickering. The other was gone. The left socket was red and bloody, a pulp of white tissue swilling softly in the black hole left behind. The energy pulsing through her had been too much for both; regretful, but this kind of thing happened.

Slowly, the one-eyed girl sat up. There was a dreadful wet squelch as she ground the heel of her bony hand into the gory socket. Flicking away a little blood and jelly, she stood. Turned, looking around herself.

Runnels of red ran down her left cheek as she smiled, forming a bloody web across half of her face.

"Black Rope," she whispered, the voice of an old woman drooling like tar from the child's mouth. The lights of the vicarage poked dimly through the trees in the distance. "What a pleasure to be here again."

PREPARATION

"I've got supplies in my car," Tilley said, "I need to go get them."

"What, more relics?" April said sardonically. "Maybe you can un-kill Hitler while you're at it. Oh, I don't know, how about a relic that raises the Earth's temperature by *another* ten degrees?"

"Look, I didn't know what you'd used the book for—"

"—and didn't ask," April snapped. "Anyway, what are you going to do? How far away is your car?"

"Back at the pub." Tilley shook his head. "It'll be fine."

"Whatever she summoned, it's out there, isn't it?"

"It'll be fine," Tilley echoed. He looked at her. The girl was clearly exhausted, her hair a mess in her face, her eyes red and raw. "Will you be okay for ten minutes?"

"You're coming back here? You're bringing whatever witch she speed-dialled—"

"—potentially witch*es*—"

"—whatever witches she speed-dialled back to my house?"

Tilley sighed. "Look, I don't want to put you in any danger. You can go. I can take you somewhere. But they're after us both now, or they will be once they know we've killed your aunt Coral. And they won't stop coming after you till they're dead or exiled from this realm. And I've seen the bone-bags you've got lying around here. This house is the best defended place for miles. You're safest here. And if you're willing, me and you could make a stand against them."

She looked at him for a long time. And then, frowning: "'Exiled from this realm'?! Christ, what are you, some kind of nineties—"

"Shut up," Tilley grumbled, patting his pockets. "I'm going to get whatever I can from the car. Take care of yourself."

The old man was halfway out into the hall when she called after him. "Will you be okay out there?"

She heard him pause, then call back, "Fine, yeah."

"You've fought witches before, right?"

"Oh, yeah. You could say that."

"Is that what the scarring's all about? Your face, it's really messed up."

No answer from the hallway.

"Is that shit going to happen to me?"

A moment, a beat, then he called back: "I'll do my best not to let anything hurt you. And I'm sorry."

"What for?"

She heard a scuffling footstep, then the front door squealed open and slammed closed behind him. April stared out into the hall for a moment, then steeled herself. She had work to do.

Outside, Tilley glanced up at the full, bloated moon and watched a plume of cool mist bloom in front of his face. "For what's about to happen," he whispered, and he headed toward the high street.

April Leek had not been practicing witchcraft for long – Christ, she would hardly call anything she'd done 'witchcraft,' but she supposed now the old man with the Hand of Michael in his pocket would tell her different – but she knew a few basic protections.

She stormed through the kitchen cupboards until she'd found a one-litre jar of rock salt. She'd never bothered too much with it when cooking, but most of the spells she'd found in the early section of Coral's book seemed to call for at least a little. She hurried into the front hall, where she was mildly annoyed to find that Tilley had tracked something that looked like soot – probably from where Aunt Coral had exploded – onto the carpet. Crouching by the front door, she poured out a thick line of salt, making sure to spray a little onto the skirting boards too. When this was done she moved to the nearest window and lined the sill. Pouring a little salt into her hand, she reached up and ground it into the metal latch. She doubted it would do much, but just in case.

Afterward she moved through the rooms, lining every door and windowsill with a thick border of salt. She had begun to run out by the time she reached the upstairs bathroom, but just had enough to create a reasonably-sized ring inside her bedroom. She could stand inside it if needed, she thought, not that any of this would do much good.

If witches can't cross it, how come you can?

"Because I'm not a witch," she told herself, returning the empty jar to the kitchen. "Not a full witch."

Not yet, maybe.

"Not ever," she reasoned, gripping the countertop as a wave of nausea hit her. The adrenaline was beginning to fade, and the fear that broiled in its wake pulsed through her like ice.

Or maybe you are. Maybe this shit just doesn't

work.

"Well then," she said, reaching for the nearest kitchen knife, "we'll have to try some other shit too."

She crossed the kitchen with the breadknife in her hand, searching for a bowl. She found one in the cupboard beside the refrigerator, only pausing very briefly to glare at the shattered plastic and ice on the tiles at her feet. She grabbed a bowl and placed it down on the counter. After a moment's hesitation, she swapped it for another. No sense in using the only *nice* bowl she had. Quickly, she rolled up her slave.

She hissed with pain as she drew the serrated blade of the breadknife across her exposed bicep. Blood beaded quickly, then formed plump drops along the thin gash she'd carved. The drops turned to runnels and dripped steadily into the bowl. Her arm stung like hell and she dropped the knife with a shaky hand, resting the blade across the top of the bowl so that any blood left on it would drop into the rest. With the same hand she squeezed her upper arm, pushing out a steady drizzle of glossy red film. She cringed. It wasn't enough. Leaning across the counter for a square of kitchen roll, she pressed it to the wound and whimpered. Dabbing hard, she said, quite stiffly: "Ow."

When she'd found a bandage and tied it crudely around her bicep, she rolled up her other sleeve and grabbed the knife with her left hand. She cut a little deeper this time, carving a matching gash on her right bicep. This one bloomed quickly and she manoeuvred it to the bowl, watching horrified as a thick stream of blood joined the rest. When it had stopped flowing so readily, she raised her arm and clamped a hand over the wound to stem the bleeding. Tying another bandage – considerably less skilfully this time – she rolled her sleeves down and grabbed the edge of the counter for support. The bowl was very full. She felt faint and dizzy.

But now the adrenaline was pumping again, thickening to mania in her slightly-emptier-than-before veins. She took the bowl and moved into the kitchen, dipping her fingers into the thick, warm liquid.

In blood she drew, from memory, an arcane protection symbol on the back of the front door. Red tracks drizzled down the wood and she drew it again, hoping it would congeal before too long. The guy renting her this place was going to kill her.

If you survive the night.

"Shut up," she said, taking the bowl deeper into the house.

When she had drawn a similar symbol on every window and door, and painted a couple of different runes on the walls that she hoped would carry a similar kind of power, she brought the empty bowl back into the kitchen and dropped it into the sink. She ran the tap for a while, but the ceramic had stained. She tried to wash her hands. Some of the darker red flaked off and swirled into the plughole, but her hands and fingers were plastered with a layer of unpleasant, rooster-feather orange that wouldn't come off. It was like the blood was baked into her flesh.

"I'll deal with you later," she whispered, turning off the tap and drying her arms. She reapplied her bandages, then headed upstairs.

Stepping over the salt line into her bedroom, she glanced at the symbol on the window: a ragged red circle crisscrossed with the *V* of an unfinished pentagram, a sigil almost like the number *3* painted inside. Then she headed over to her desk, where the Undoing Knife stood buried in the skin-bound book.

She sat in the chair and curled her fingers around the knife, still feeling slightly faint. When she had managed to get a strong enough grip on the handle, she pulled. There was an awful meaty smell as the knife released itself from the pages, and a thin wisp of black sooty smoke rose from the wound. She dropped it onto the table.

She read for a while, beginning to think that ten minutes must have passed, that Tilley should be back by now. She had started reading with the hopes of discovering or translating some new spell, something useful, but she read more feverishly as she felt an intense need to distract herself.

After twenty minutes or so there was a knock on the

front door downstairs, the second one tonight.

April froze.

Tilley moved quietly through the centre of Black Rope, following a sparsely-moonlit path toward the inn. The houses seemed taller now, their shadows falling longer and more solidly across the high street. The trees swelling up the sloping sides of the valley were pointed claws grasping for him. The night was dark and the air tingling with the electricity of an oncoming storm.

As he neared the Catch Dog he heard something barking from the direction of the high street and remembered the couple he'd seen walking their greyhound-cross earlier in the evening. Momentarily he considered doubling back, warning them to get inside and stay there; if the witch's coven had been called in, then the whole village was in danger. If the Parliament were here, God forbid, then the danger would be amplified a thousandfold. But he was close to the car now, and his equipment. He moved across the gravel car park in the shadow of the inn, flickering amber light riding his back. He glanced toward the elderly couple's table as he reached the car. Nobody there, just a pair of empty glasses and an abandoned pack of cards.

"Shit," he whispered. No, he was sure they'd just gone inside the inn, or perhaps home. If something had happened to them – to anyone – he wouldn't be able to forgive himself. How could he have been so stupid? He was right, of course, it was procedure to destroy the book, not to question – or at least to destroy first and ask questions later – but maybe procedure was wrong. Maybe it wasn't just him that was getting a little too old for this; maybe the Agency needed to update their rulebook. If people like April existed now – people who had fallen into witchcraft through no fault of their own, people whose only crime was ridding the world of another, more significant threat like the girl's aunt – then they had existed for all time. The rulebook had always been wrong.

He popped the car boot and it squealed as he flung it open.

Of course, the witchfinders of old had mostly been wrong. That dick Hopkins and his crew; the Germans; the mob up in Lancashire… ninety-nine per cent of the witches accused and punished and extinguished throughout history had been innocent. Outcasts, some of them, but not criminals. Not witches.

But the Agency was supposed to be different. They had always hunted the real monsters, magic-abusers who had hurt and killed and become abominable…

How many people like April had *he* killed? How many that didn't deserve it?

This wasn't the first time he'd questioned everything. And he only had the girl's word to go off.

What if she was lying? What if she was just like Aunt Coral – working with her, maybe – or worse?

He looked down as he reached into the Tasmin's boot and saw that his hand was shaking. "They're all the same," he told himself. Even the girl had played a part in this, willing or not. And once he'd finished with whoever Coral had summoned to Black Rope, he would deal with her. The BWFA weren't like the witchfinders who had prosecuted and executed with no reason, no cause; in fact, they had largely been established to fight those frauds as well as any *actual* witches they encountered. He wouldn't have been a part of it all if he thought they were acting with undue prejudice. "They *are* all the same. You're just getting old. You're going soft, Jack."

He rummaged in the case and collected a few items and relics, planting them about his person. Most he stuffed into his pockets; a couple he threw around his neck.

He slammed the lid closed, then turned and looked toward the inn. The narrow windows betrayed no movement inside, only the flickering of gas lamps. The place was an eerily-quiet shell. Tilley fumbled in his pocket for his phone, suddenly remembering that procedure in a situation like this required him to contact the Agency for backup. He was hesitant to let Elena find out he'd gotten Black Rope into this mess, but it was the right thing to do.

Better not fuck this up twice over, he thought. Not unless he wanted the BWFA to enforce his retirement before he'd made the decision himself.

He swore to himself; there were no bars. Of course not. He'd had signal in his room at the inn though, he remembered, and quickly he crossed the parking lot toward the front door. Again he glanced up at the sign, shuddering at the gruesome hunting scene depicted there in garish bloody paint. He opened the door and stepped inside.

"Hello?" Tilley called quietly as he withdrew from the shadow of the vestibule and into the empty bar. Hayley was gone from behind the counter, and he was mildly concerned to note that Johnny and Mary, the old couple from outside, were nowhere to be seen either. The enormous stag skull above the bar glared at him with its hollow, black eyes between shelves of glinting glasses. "Hayley? You around?"

It was just late, he decided, heading across the bar and toward the stairs. She'd gone to bed with the rest of them.

And all the lights still on?

He ignored the tiny voice and headed upstairs, checking his phone again before padding over the landing toward his room. Still nothing, though a single service bar flickered at the top of the stairs before dying again, which was vaguely encouraging.

Jack Tilley unlocked the door to his room and

stepped inside. Everything was as he'd left it, only now bathed in a speckled blanket of moonlight filtering in through the window. In the dim blue glare he went to the window and raised his phone high, hoping the extra storey would be enough.

"Gotcha," he whispered as two bars flickered on the display, then solidified. He started to dial.

The screen blackened suddenly, the display shrinking to a vortex of dead pixels before extinguishing completely. The bedroom lights flickered on, flaring a brilliant white and making him cringe, then died again with a small explosion of shattering glass. Behind him the door blew open, flung into the wall with a crash. Tilley wheeled around to see a silhouette in the doorway, the phone dead in his hand.

Hayley smiled thinly as the landing lights flashed. Her face was dark, her eyes bristling with yellow.

"Hi," Tilley said. He gestured vaguely with the phone. "I was just trying to… ah, you don't care, do you?"

The landlady grinned, teeth flashing in the dark.

"Thought not."

POSSESSION

April stalked slowly down the stairs, her arms throbbing where she had cut them open above the elbows. Whoever had knocked on the door a moment ago was quiet now; she heard nothing as she reached the hall, nothing as she backed into the kitchen – keeping her eyes on the door all the while – and fumbled for the breadknife. There was an awful scrape of metal on ceramic as she removed it from the sink, gripping the handle tight. Just in case.

The last time somebody had knocked on the door, a witch-hunter had stormed into her house and tried to kill her before bringing Aunt Coral back to life. And breaking her freezer.

This time she was going to be prepared.

Back in the hall, she paused. For a full minute she stood at the bottom of the stairs, breathing as quietly as she could. Her chest was sore with anticipation, blood pumping loudly in her ears. The knife trembled, her knuckles white and bulging.

A single bead of her own blood slid down the serrated blade to its point and dripped slowly onto the carpet.

KNOCK KNOCK KNOCK

She winced, almost jumping out of her skin at the sound. Whoever was out there really wanted to get in.

Slowly, April Leek moved across the hall, tightening her grip on the kitchen knife and tucking her arm behind her back. She flexed her fingers, reaching out with her free hand to open the door. The breadknife felt wrong in her palm; she switched hands, drawing a sharp intake of breath. Her fingers hovered around the doorhandle.

KNOCK KNOCK KNOCK

"Who is it?" she called. Her voice drifted weakly into the hall and died. There was no answer.

Swallowing, April grabbed the handle and twisted.

The door swung open and she stepped forward, preparing to whip her arm out from behind her back and swipe at her attacker's face. For a moment she thought she might've imagined it all – there was no one there – and then she lowered her eyes.

Nora stood on the doorstep, her face bathed in shadow.

"Oh," April said, stepping back. The kid had walked all the way here from the park where April had found her on the swings; her shins were smeared with dirt and there was a waxy green leaf plastered to one shoe. April lowered the knife. It flashed at her side. "Hey, honey. Oh, hey, sorry, don't worry about this. I was just… it doesn't matter. Do you need to come in?"

The girl nodded, not lifting her head. Her hair was in her eyes, darkness painting her brow and filling the sockets either side of her nose.

"Is it Mummy and Daddy? They fighting?" April said, glancing out into the street. "Come in, love, it's okay. You'll be safe in here."

Safer in here than out there, she thought, looking left and right before opening the door wide. Her heel scuffed the salt line as she stepped back to let Nora inside.

"That's it, honey. Head upstairs, yeah? I'll get you a drink and we'll have a little talk, see if we need to…"

April shut the door and looked in Nora's direction. The girl was standing still in the hall, not six feet from her, her little head lowered. She sniffed.

"Everything okay?" April said hesitantly.

Slowly, the girl turned her head and looked up.

April gasped, clamping a hand over her mouth.

Nora's cheeks were puffy and red, probably from the cold, her nose was running with blood, thin streams of it flowing slowly into her mouth. Her left eye was gone, a gory hole tunnelling into her skull. Jelly drizzled down her cheek.

Nora smiled, then sniffed again. Deeply. "She was here…" the girl whispered. She grinned wickedly. "You don't look happy to see me. Why is that?"

April's grip tightened again. A thick gob of blood-pulp slithered out of the child's eye-socket and streamed down her face to her neck.

Tilley stood in the centre of the room, the dead phone snapped closed in his palm. He kept his eyes locked on Hayley as she swayed gently in the doorway, her silhouetted head and neck haloed by the flickering light from out on the landing. Her fingers were dug into the wood in the frame.

"Evening," he said quietly.

He flinched as the landlady stepped forward, noting a splotchy scarf of flesh encircling her throat: the skin was pinched and blistered as if she'd been scratching it for some time. Glossy red pinpricks scattered her broken throat. The rash continued up her cheeks and around her ears and eyes, which were streaked through with thin black veins like something had burst. Her right knee was bent back a little and she took an awkward step, wobbling as she entered the room as though she wasn't sure where to distribute the weight of her own body. The skin around her eyes sagged.

"You're hurting her, aren't you?" Tilley asked, his gaze returning to the violent rash blossoming across her neck. "The woman you're possessing. She can't cope with it."

Hayley – the thing in Hayley's body, anyway – ignored him, taking another janky step forward.

"You need to let her go," Tilley growled. "Her body isn't strong enough to contain your spirit. You know that. And what happens to you when she runs out? Where do you go?"

The Hayley-thing smiled a little, teeth flashing again. Her gums were bleeding.

"Okay, you're not letting her go. Fine. Tell me who you are."

Nothing.

"Tell me *what* you are. Just another witch? Or one of them?"

The thing in Hayley's body cocked one of her eyebrows.

"You are," Tilley nodded, slowly trying to move his hand to his coat pocket. He would have to be fast. "You're one of the Parliament, aren't you? Well, okay. I was hoping Coral didn't have particularly strong connections, but I guess she's got friends in high places. *Had* friends in high places. Sorry"—Hayley's face had twisted into a spiteful snarl—"I should know better than to remind someone like you that one of your number is dead."

The door slammed behind the Hayley-thing and she lurched toward him again. The room was almost completely dark, but he could see the tiny yellow points in the centre of each eye, swirling around each other in a writhing vortex.

"So are you all here?" Tilley said, dipping the pads of his fingers into his coat. "All seven of you?"

No response, just a faint growl.

"Wouldn't it be fun to be the man who took out the entire Parliament of Witches?" Tilley mused aloud. "Then I could retire. You know, I hope all seven of you *have* come, then I can wipe every stinking piss-eyed witch off the face of the—"

"You know of us," Hayley whispered finally, her voice hoarse and not her own.

Tilley's teeth set in his jaw.

"We know of you too," the Hayley-thing spat, then she screamed forward through the dark.

10

TURNING THE BLOOD

The knife felt suddenly very heavy in her hand.

Nora gazed up at her, one-eyed, the child's mouth a thin curve. Tiny yellow spots danced a slow circle around her remaining pupil. Her skin was blotchy in places, April saw, and her body twitched occasionally as though on the edge of a seizure. This wasn't the same child April had met in the park earlier that night. But she was still a child. And as frightened as April was of the one-eyed thing wearing Nora's flesh, she couldn't attack a child with a breadknife.

"Coward," the Nora-thing hissed, as if reading her thoughts. "Why don't you run, then, coward? Why don't you run away—"

April barrelled past her and onto the stairs, her heart hammering her chest as she thundered up them two at a time. She cringed as the not-child shrieked with laughter behind her, a sick rattling exploding from Nora's lungs. At the top of the stairs April wheeled round, backing up on the landing toward her bedroom and wielding the breadknife.

Her eyes widened as she watched the not-child rise into the air.

"That's it," said the thing molesting Nora's voice, grinning as it spread its child-hands and levitated two feet, three, from the carpet, feet dangling, toes pointing down as it climbed into the air. "Run, bitch. Witch-killer. Run and give me something to chase…"

April dashed across the landing to her bedroom, scrambling for the door as the not-child flew into the air, bypassing the stairs and twisting herself over the banister. April screamed, looking back as the door swung open to see Nora's body turned in on itself and moving on hands and feet, crab-like, toward her, jaws snapping like some mad piranha. "Fucking hell," she yelled, rushing into the room and slamming the door. The not-child smashed into the wood and April ran for the writing desk, fumbling with the pages of the open book. There must be something in here, something basic, something she could use…

The door slammed open before April could even

find the spell that might turn the not-child into a snake. April yelled out again as some invisible force coiled around her waist and yanked her across the room, slamming her hard into the wall beside her window. Moonlight thrust into the room as she struggled, her feet dangling inches off the ground, her back pressed hard into the plaster. It had cracked around her with the force. Her eyes turned down to the not-child crawling into the room.

"What are you?" April screamed, invisible hands squeezing her throat and chest, pinning her flailing legs to the wall. She could feel phantom fingers digging into her fist, trying to pry it open and release her grip of the knife. More in her mouth trying to rip out her tongue. She clamped her teeth down hard.

"Why, I'm just a little girl," said the not-child, extending its neck. Nora's lower jaw dropped slack suddenly, a gaping black pit opening in her face, and inside April saw a thick, pointed worm of a tongue – red and lumpen, like a turkey's neck – poking at her teeth. Her single eye flashed, another bead of blood oozing from the hole where the left had been. "I can smell her memories… oh, Mummy was so *cruel* to this one. Daddy too."

The not-child grinned, her slack jaw curling up into a yawing crescent. The tongue inside thrashed and writhed.

"She really thought you were going to save her."

April yelled as the not-child scuttled across the room toward her, leering up suddenly and slamming a foot into her knee. April's leg buckled and she dropped to the floor with a gasp as the invisible hands released her, then the not-child dug a tiny hand into her neck and pressed the fingers hard into her jugular. April wheezed, flinging up her arm and swiping with the knife. The not-child grabbed her wrist and twisted and April felt the knife dropping from suddenly-useless fingers, felt a bolt of pain from wrist to elbow. With her free hand she scrambled on the windowsill above them. "Fuck off!" she yelled, grabbing a leathery bag from the sill and slamming it into the not-child's mouth.

The Nora-thing squalled as April slammed her slack jaw into her teeth, locking the bag inside. The leathery thing contained all manner of powders and chicken bones and had been blessed with a protective spell that – she had thought, at least – was meant to keep evil out of the house. Well, perhaps it would do a little better in the thing's throat.

Temporarily released, April lurched to her feet and stepped over the convulsing, wriggling not-child, stumbling toward the writing desk. She grabbed the book and slammed it closed, holding it tight against her chest. She looked to the window, where the not-child was gagging and wheezing, back arched. April turned to the door.

Before she could take a step the not-child appeared in front of the bedroom door in a blur of flesh and blood, wiping its mouth and smiling sickly. "Not so fast," it rasped.

April changed course, barrelling toward the window. Wheeling around on one heel, she slammed her back into the glass and tipped herself up over the sill. Glass shattered in a spray of iridescent shards all around her and she screamed as something sliced her cheek open, tumbling heels over head and gripping the book to her chest as she was launched through the broken frame and into the night.

Tilley ducked to the side as the thing in the landlady's body hurled itself at him, clawing at the air with a gnarled hand. He lashed out and grabbed Hayley's wrist, bone crackling somewhere in her arm as the flesh of her wrist flaked drily beneath his fingers, motes of skin flecking the air. "Get off me!" she rasped, her elbow shooting up into his arm. Her head whipped around suddenly and she bared her teeth. Tilley balled his free hand into a fist and rabbit-punched her in the nose.

A soft spray of red warmth painted Hayley's face and Tilley let go of her arm, stumbling backward as the thing inside grabbed at its host body's broken nose.

"You imp!" the Hayley-thing wheezed, snarling and

turning toward him. She clocked Tilley's hand poking around in his jacket and shot forward, a streak of fury and rage. Before he could duck out of the way she headbutted his jaw, a hard dome of bone smashing into his teeth. He crumpled into the wardrobe, shoulder slamming the wood. Something had cracked open in his mouth. His eyes snapped open wide as he saw the angry streak of the Hayley-thing blurring toward him again and instinctively he kicked out, punching his boot into her thigh. Hayley's body buckled and the thing inside her screeched with her lungs, fresh blisters cracking open on her cheeks and neck under the strain. "Enough, imp! Cower before me!"

Tilley cocked an eyebrow, gurning as warmth filled his mouth. He reached up to wipe blood from his lips and flung droplets of it into the carpet, balling both hands into fists. "You don't have to talk like fucking Othello, you know, just because you're a—"

The Hayley-creature shrieked, launching herself at him again. Tilley yelled as she snapped her teeth at his throat, a monstrous wet tongue punching at his jugular. Grabbing her by the shoulders, he slammed the landlady's body into the wardrobe and backed up, heading for the bed as he reached into his pocket.

"You know me," Tilley called as the Hayley-thing turned her head to glower at him and the smell of sulphur blossomed into the room. "You said you know me. You must know how many witches I've killed."

"If you think us mere witches," the thing smiled, flexing both arms with a series of dry, bony pops, "you have no concept of the power of our Parliament. We are ancient, Jonathan. Ancient and hungry. Starved by the aeons and formed of the hatred of ages. You are *nothing* to us."

A blast of cold air slammed into his gut and he fell onto the bed, knocking the back of his skull against the wall. His fingers curled tightly around something in his pocket.

"You are *all* nothing to us," the thing hissed, spreading both of Hayley's hands into rigid claws. It rose into the air, floating to the ceiling and advancing slowly toward him until it was hovering inches from where he lay sprawled and heaving on the mattress. "We could destroy you all."

Tilley opened his mouth to speak, but something twisted tightly in his throat.

"How can you possibly fight something," the Hayley-thing whispered, "that can turn your own blood against you?"

He felt it then, coursing through him: every blood cell bristled suddenly, his veins snapping taut as the fluid thickened. He gasped, unable to speak, struggling to breathe, his heart pumping four or five times its normal speed as the creature grinned above him, twisting Hayley's wrists as if controlling and manipulating some invisible set of puppet-strings. Her fingers spread wide and he felt streams of blood twist around themselves, clotting his arteries, felt an intense surge of heat as the blood cells began to bubble, broiling and sizzling and flooding him with pressure—

"No," he gasped, and he withdrew his arm from his coat. His joints were stiff, the blood in his limbs heating and curdling, every fibre of his being screaming with agony. With all the energy he had left he surged to his feet on the bed and thrust up his arm.

The jawbone in his hand had once belonged to John Hathorne. It was the only part of him, Tilley thought grimly as he punched the ragged-toothed curve of bone into Hayley's throat, that would ever do any good to anyone.

Blood winged from Hayley's jugular and she fell onto the bed, the thing inside her clawing at the gaping wound in her neck. Her eyes rolled up in her head as Tilley scrambled out of reach and across the room, leaving the jawbone firmly buried in her windpipe. He glanced back as he reached the door; blood sprayed the bed and the wall, a spatter of red painting the plaster as the Hayley-thing squealed and writhed.

Swallowing, he slammed the door and lurched across the landing, tumbling down the stairs and into the inn. His body was stiff and cold, his blood suddenly released from the creature's grip and cooling fast, the popped blood cells lost for good and leaving him feeling drained and exhausted. He struggled past the bar, fumbling in his pockets as he headed for the front door of the Catch Door.

"Not so fast," something rasped off to his left. He turned his head to see the old man from earlier that night, sitting at one of the previously-empty tables by the fire. The hearth was lit, logs popping wetly in a blue-hot curtain of flame that sent ribbons of smoke up into the flue. The heat coming from the fire was strong and greasy.

"Johnny," Tilley wheezed.

"Is that what I was called?" the old man said slowly, his voice crackling and dirty. "I forget, you see, these tired old things have names…"

His eyes sparkled, yellow points flashing around the edges of the pupils. He looked across the bar, past Tilley's shoulder.

"What was hers, do you think?"

Tilley turned to see Mary – or the thing wearing her body – sitting at another table across the bar from him. "Oh, not you too," he breathed.

Mary smiled, raising a withered hand to wave cheerily at him. Her eyes shone.

Tilley flexed his fingers, his knuckles popping as he balled his hands into fists. His chest was still heaving, heart ricocheting off his ribs so fast that he was starting to worry he might actually go into cardiac arrest. He had avoided it this far, despite everything; it would be nice, he thought, to take a few minutes and regulate his heartbeat.

The elderly couple had other ideas.

"What shall we do to him?" the Johnny-thing rasped, climbing out of his chair and curling his knotted knuckles around the edge of the table. It cricked his neck loudly, grinning with crooked teeth.

"Shall we skin him?"

"I'd like to flay him," the Mary-thing said, rising to her feet.

"Lash him," the Johnny-thing agreed, "flog him, whip him, beat him."

"*Peel* him," the Mary-thing whispered.

Tilley swallowed, glancing from one to the other and then to the door, calculating the distance between the gruesomely-smirking hosts and himself, then the distance to the exit… he doubted he had the strength to fight them both, not at his age, not after the Hayley-thing had put so much strain on his body, not now that his heart was pounding, thumping, slamming—

"Burn him," the Johnny-thing decided.

The Mary-thing smiled.

Tilley took a slow step back toward the bar, his mind dropped into overdrive, frantically punching through the options as the elderly hosts stepped toward him, closing the distance. He felt a sudden surge of wet, almost-pleasant heat and glanced toward the fireplace to see that the flames had grown to thick bright tongues in the hearth. Beside him the thing in Mary's body raised her wrinkled hand and stretched the fingers.

"How much heat do you think he can stand?" she whispered.

"Oh, not much," Johnny said. "These bodies are so… weak."

Tilley shook his head. "So are yours," he said. "You don't want to do this."

There was a soft *whoomph* and the flames surged again, devouring the stone edges of the fireplace as Mary twisted her wrist. The logs crackled, almost invisible now through the wall of shimmering heat filling the hearth.

"These bodies don't matter," Mary said, smiling gleefully. Her old rheumy eyes sparkled with hunger. "You can do what you like to them, old man, but you won't hurt us. We're tucked up nice and safe in here. Protected. And if we have to leave them for some other body…"

"Thought so," Tilley said grimly. "Just wanted to check."

"You can't hurt us," Johnny whispered.

"We won't be killed," Mary giggled.

"Why?" Tilley said desperately. The thing in Mary's body clenched her fingers tight and the fire roared, flames shooting out of the hearth and embracing the nearest table. A streak of orange shot up the leg and started to lick at the edge of the table's surface, quickly enveloping a cardboard pint coaster. "Why do this? Witches die all the time. Trust me, I've killed a lot of them. Why avenge this one?"

"She called us," the Johnny-thing snarled. "We are bound."

"And we *willingly* accept," the Mary-thing said,

extending her second hand. The hearth had become a swirling centre of fire, the stones around it charred black, the carpet catching. The heat was incredible. "We are not so often… called to action, these days. We *miss* it."

Tilley was beginning to sweat. The elderly couple had closed in again – there was hardly six feet between him and not-Johnny now, even less between him and the old man's not-wife. The door seemed further away than ever.

Another table caught, flames lashing the legs and chairs. A wall of fire crackled around the outer edge of the bar, heading slowly for him. Sweat plastered his back, heat spreading across his face and neck. His heart was going six beats a second. Somewhere outside, he heard the distant sound of a dog barking. He reached up to tug at his collar. Sweat drizzled into his shirt, more of it running between the lumpen masses of scar tissue scattering his bald head.

"All right," he said to himself, looking again toward the front door. "Nothing to lose by trying—"

The door swung open suddenly and April burst in, clutching something to her chest with one hand. She was out of breath and her hair was a mess, matted with blood and stained green. Flakes of glass shone in the tangles around her face, more of it on her clothes. She clocked the two old hosts and her gaze landed on Tilley. "What the hell is going on in here?"

The fire roared again as the Mary-thing turned her neck in April's direction, tightening both fists. Great tongues of flame leapt out of the hearth and coiled around the nearby tables. At the back of the restaurant a curtain caught suddenly, flames barrelling up the window. "Get out of here!" Tilley yelled.

"What—"

"*This* one, I'm going to skin," the Johnny-thing said.

April's eyes widened and she raised a hand suddenly, spreading her fingers outward. She whispered something unintelligible and Tilley watched, amazed, as the fire in the hearth was briefly strangled. The heat dropped immediately by a few degrees and he lurched forward, stumbling across the bar toward her. "That's it," he whispered, "keep going—"

"Nice try," Mary rasped, and the thing controlling her body snapped her fingers. Fire shot out of the hearth in streams and April yelled, backing up and dropping her hand. Tilley grabbed her shoulders.

"Fucking hell!" April coughed, slamming the book into Tilley's hand and pushing both her palms outward. For a moment Tilley thought she might actually win out: the fire seemed to shrivel on itself and sink back toward the fireplace, the flames streaming across the burning tables quenched into pillars of black smoke. Then he heard the Mary-thing laughing and a wall of heat punched through the Catch Dog, more fire rolling across the carpet. "It's not working! What do I do?"

Before Tilley could answer, she turned her attention to the back of the bar, where the stag skull mounted on the wall watched them blankly from between rows and rows of bottles.

"Get down!" she yelled, and she wheeled her hands toward the bar.

"Wait," Tilley said, "what are you—"

His eyes widened as he realised what she was doing and he ducked, pulling her down with him. There was a beat and then a titanic scream of shattering glass as April clamped her fingers into tight fists, shrieking something in Latin. Tilley watched in horror as every bottle on the wall exploded, glass spraying the walls, gallons of vodka and rum and other spirits detonating in a wall of glittering liquid droplets. Spirits flooded the fire and the flames unfolded into thick, yellow pylons of heat, shooting into every corner of the bar. Tilley yanked April back and kicked open the door with his shoulder, shoving them both through as fire roared through the Catch Dog, filling the windows with greasy roiling clouds of amber.

"Christ!" he yelled, staggering back across the gravel with her. "You okay?"

"I'm fine!" April said, grabbing the book back from him. "Come on!"

Behind them the door of the pub swung open and

the Johnny-thing staggered out, his flesh boiled and blackened, blisters cascading over his face and neck as flames rode his back and shoulders. Tilley heard the Mary-thing screeching inside.

"Your place?" Tilley said.

"Not safe," April panted.

"Okay," Tilley said, grabbing her hand. "This way, then."

The windows of the Catch Dog exploded as they ran across the gravel toward the high street, tongues of fire punching out into the night with an intense spray of heat that reminded Tilley, just for a second, of the place deep in the earth that these creatures had come from.

12

BONES

Hayley's body stirred in the old man's bed.

The bone was wedged firmly in the flesh of her jaw, blood steadily pouring down her neck in thick red runnels. The sheets were a mess of slimy gore. Her eyes flickered open. The thing inside her exhaled, and a plume of sooty black trailed out of the host body's mouth.

Slowly, the thing sat up.

It reached up, manipulating Hayley's fingers with a stiff sort of crookedness. It cupped the shelf of her jaw and curled her hand around the bone, smiling thinly as warmth spread into the cracks of its borrowed palm.

Blood ran between the fingers as it pulled, gripping the crooked jawbone tight and unsheathing it from the flesh of Hayley's neck. A fresh wing of wet, ropey red sprayed the sheets and she wheezed. The bone fell to the floor at her feet. The thing stretched Hayley's fingers, cricking her neck, and tipped up her head. A wall of shining blood slid down her throat.

Her eyes flickered, then blazed a searing electric yellow.

"Mother," the thing whispered. Hayley's voice was unrecognisable: gurgling and hollow, blood bubbling over her lips. Her eyes flashed, bright sparks dancing across tiny, pinprick pupils. Her body twitched as she sat on the edge of the bed, hands splayed at either side of her. Below her there was a fantastic heat; from outside, thin trails of smoke rolled through the door. The fire would reach her soon.

Across town, inside the old vicarage, the creature inside Nora's body tilted back its own borrowed head. Her eyes burned. "Speak," she hissed.

"My vessel is weak," the thing said with Hayley's tongue, now slick and red. Warmth filled her windpipe. Her chest was covered with it now. "Breaking. I seek permission."

The girl-thing in the old vicarage turned her head toward the window, looking across the fields toward the Catch Dog. The fire in her eyes rippled as they communed. "You wish to come through fully?"

"If I may."

"You will not be harmed if your vessel is destroyed," the girl-thing reminded her. Her voice entered the Hayley-creature's head directly, a whisper passing through bone. "Coming through, you risk your true form."

Hayley spat bitterly, blood clotting the saliva. "They can't hurt me. not if I am allowed to fight with my real hands."

"Your vessel serves a purpose," Nora's disembodied voice echoed softly.

"If this feeble body burns," the Hayley-thing said, "I will be returned to my own. It will take me some time to find another vessel and return to the fight. If I may, I would rather remain."

"You have always longed for blood," the child sighed. "I presume you cannot be convinced otherwise?"

"I will do as you wish, Mother."

The child paused, seeming to think. The thing inside nodded Nora's head, eventually. "Permission granted. Come through."

Hayley grinned. The light in her eyes flickered and died.

She stood, slowly, stepping over the discarded bloody jawbone. Her spine cracked loudly as it straightened. For a moment the room was quiet, save for the crackling of fire below and the creaking of the timber; this place would fall through and cave in in a few minutes. She didn't need that long.

The thing whispered something unintelligible, something alien, the sounds forming in the sharp curls of Hayley's tongue and escaping before her teeth could trap them. She spread her arms and her body seized, stiffening suddenly as faint red trails of smoke formed a crude upside-down star behind her.

A dreadful wet crack echoed out of her mouth, followed by more pops and cracks all across her body. Her joints bent and splintered as her skeleton was turned inside-out, knobs and plates of bone punching up against her flesh before sinking away again. Hayley's stomach deflated and she howled, agony coursing through her legs and arms as they tightened, stretched from the inside.

Then the witch began to come through.

Hayley's pores smouldered as the wizened body of the creature pushed through her flesh, bones snapping outward, her skin sloughing off in bloody sheets as the thing writhed and bucked; it surged out of her with one final rend of flesh, organs popping wetly and drizzling down the witch's body.

It stood in the pulp of Hayley's bloody clothes and skin, its chest rising and falling as it gathered itself. It was a little taller than she had been, and far more slender, crusty grey skin clinging to every bone so that its figure was terrifyingly skeletal. It was bald and its gums were raw and wet, mouth open in a long, ecstatic gasp. Its eyes were tiny yellow points in their deep, pit-like sockets; it had no nose, but two ragged black holes ridged with bone where a nose might have been. It stretched, its fingers cracking loudly: long, rake-like things that sprung from a collection of knuckles too numerous to belong in each hand. A mess of blood and organic, pinkish fluid seeped down through cracks in the creature's skin, which looked burned and sticky to touch. Sharp black bristles rose from its shoulders and chest, quivering.

The witch left Tilley's room silently, moving like a ghost. Its hips were angular and jutted from a narrow spindle of a waist; its legs were like branches. Fire had spread up the stairs and the landing was unbearably hot. The thing walked calmly to the staircase and began descending into the wet, orange warmth. Flames retreated from it. Smoke roiled across the ceiling, black plumes filling every corner of the landing.

The inn crumbled around the witch as it stepped out into the bar, untouched by the fire. Great walls of flame pressed up to the edges of the ceiling, roaring and bellowing. The floor was a ruin of pulsing carpet-flames, the tables ablaze. The spirit bottles on the wall had shattered, and millions of tiny glass pieces crackled with hot yellow life.

The thing caught sight of itself in a broken, curved shard of glass and hissed. Its face was repugnant, almost goblin-like, wrinkles and cracks betraying the creature's impossible age.

Slowly, it turned its head.

Hung on the wall behind the bar was the titanic skull of a stag, its antlers licked by ribbons of white fire. Its eye sockets blazed.

The thing smiled, moving calmly to the skull and gripping it by the antlers. With an unearthly strength it wrenched the hunting trophy from the wall and blew softly. Immediately the flames consuming the skull were extinguished, leaving blossoms of smoke rising from the eye sockets. For a moment she stared into the deep black tunnels, smiling thinly.

Then, lifting the skull with both hands, she turned it around and brought it to her own face. Withered grey skin fused with bone, the two knitting together, leech-like points of flesh snapping to the edges of the skull.

The witch turned, looking into the blazing heart of the Catch Dog. Its shadow fell upon the far wall, a glorious crown of twisted, gnarled antlers rising from its silhouetted head.

"So they're not normal witches, right?" April panted as they tore down the high street. The tall shadows of the pine trees surrounding the village quivered in the wind. She clutched the book in her arms, pressed to her chest, her legs aching already. "They're the Parliament you were talking about. Right? Normal witches don't possess little girls, do they?"

"Oh, any witch is capable of projecting their spirit into another body," Tilley said, slowing to a stagger as he paused to scramble for his breath. The girl slowed to match his pace, glancing behind them in the direction of the inn – little more, now, than a faint bead of orange in the trees. The old man continued: "But yes, that's the Parliament. The one in the kid is called Mother. The rest are her daughters."

"Actual daughters, or weird cult daughters?"

"Either," Tilley shrugged. "Both. Doesn't matter. They're too dangerous."

"What do we do?" she said, lurching into a jog as Tilley sped up again, holding a hand to his side. His bootheels clapped the pavement loudly. "How are they doing it? Can we get them out of those people?"

"There are seven of them," Tilley breathed, slowing again and shaking his head. "We have to walk, sorry. I'm too old for this shit."

"We're fine," she said, looking back again. Nobody seemed to have followed them from the inn, but she couldn't help but see shapes in every shadow.

"Seven of them. They will have possessed seven bodies. Any damage we do to them will only damage the bodies themselves. Kill the host, and the witch doesn't die, it just goes back to its own body."

"And where is that?"

"Nobody knows," he shook his head. "The Agency has tried to find the Parliament before, and no luck. Somewhere underground, that's usually where you'll find a witch's nest."

"So we can't do anything without killing the people they're possessing. Nora…"

"There are ways of forcing them out, but we're going to have to use our resources wisely. Best thing to do for now is to regroup somewhere safe and rest for a minute. Christ, my ribs. You can run ahead, you know. I'll catch up."

"What do you mean 'out'?"

"Back to their bodies. Or…"

"Or?"

"Once a witch – at least, a witch as powerful as these ones – has possessed something, then it has a psychic connection with the mind it's settled down in. They can use those connections like cables – fibre optics, I guess – travel through them—"

"You're saying they can come here properly."

"Yes. It's cruel magic, but it works. Any of the seven could choose to exit their host body at any time, and if they do, they'll be a dozen times more powerful. A witch in its own skin is a nightmare, but a Parliament of witches who've decided their hosts aren't strong enough? We're not going to make it out of here alive."

April paused. She stood in the middle of the road, suddenly still, and grabbed his arm. "Okay. But if they come through—"

"Yes," he said. "If they come through, if they come *here*, they can be killed."

"So we force them out of the hosts," April said.

He shook his head. "The hosts would die."

"We trap them somehow—"

"Then they come through of their own volition. Hosts die."

"Okay, so we—"

"Hosts die," Tilley said grimly.

"Or—"

"Hosts. Die."

"So what do we do?" April asked, her eyes wide.

Tilley hesitated. Eventually he opened his mouth.

Before he could get a word out, the powerful barking of a dog boomed across the street. The old man wheeled around, eyes flitting from shadow to shadow until they landed on a shape lurching toward them from the end of the road. Three shapes.

"Shit," Tilley whispered.

The dog-walkers from earlier. The brown-haired woman in the coat and scarf and her husband, both of their eyes flickering a dim yellow. Between them, off his lead and practically foaming at the mouth, the German Shepherd cross stalked powerfully forward, shoulders rolled back, teeth bared.

"More witches?" April whispered.

"More witches," Tilley nodded, swallowing.

***

A dense miasma of blood-red fog swirled slowly around the vicarage, bright points of light storming through clouds of clotted crimson. The roiling fog moved snake-like in depressive circles, seeping across the ground and rolling up into itself.

The Nora-thing watched the street from the upstairs window, her face pressed to the glass. Her eyes reflected the red sparks in the mist, her expression stony and calm.

Something approached the house across the adjacent field. Slowly the thing in the girl's body turned its borrowed head, smiling thinly at the oncoming creature. Down below, the witch with the great stag's skull fused to its face looked up, the antlers tipping back, yellow fires burning inside the eye sockets. The creature's body was wrinkled and malnourished beyond comprehension, so bony and shrivelled that it looked alien. It spread its hands, long bent fingers stretching into stars.

"Enter," the Nora-thing whispered, and the stag-headed thing nodded in appreciation. The door to the vicarage swung open, a narrow valley opening in the fog. The creature stalked forward, dragging its fingers through the parted mist-walls.

Upstairs, the girl's eyes flashed yellow.

"Daughters," she whispered, "do you hear me?"

In a blazing corner of the Catch Dog, a wrinkled black shape that had once been named Mary twitched, lights flickering weakly on inside its burned skull. Fires leapt all around the thing as its mouth opened, strings of charred flesh separating wetly. "Mother…"

Just outside, the scorched body of Mary's husband knelt in the gravel, clothes fused to his flesh, blood streaming from blistered skin. The thing inside him tipped back his head, eyes lighting up. "Mother, speak to us."

"Come through," the Nora-thing said. "Join your sister."

The Johnny-thing grinned, teeth flashing in its blackened mouth. Immediately the old man's body began to buck and twist, bones exploding outward, and the witch-creature punched its way out of him, angular joints flexing, cracking loudly. It screeched as Johnny's flesh and insides ran off its body in wet, thick walls. Inside the bar the Mary-thing yowled as the host body was sloughed off, another skeletal, narrow shape twisting out of her.

Slowly, they stood. The thing that had broken free of Johnny's broken body turned its head toward the door and smiled as it opened. The second creature stepped out, flat feet slapping the gravel, toes gnarled and twisted around each other. The pub burned.

Together, the creatures headed toward the vicarage.

13

DEWORM

Tilley stepped forward, both of his hands raised in front of his chest. Behind him, April swallowed. "It's all right," the old man said quietly, his eyes flitting from the woman to her husband then finally to the dog and back again. "We'll come. Let's just take this somewhere else, shall we?"

The woman snarled, doglike, her lips peeling back. Her eyes sparkled with malice. The crossbreed grinned at her heels, ears stiff and pointed, the same hungry light winking in each of his eyes. The woman's husband stood lopsided, one shoulder dipped beneath the other, a blank, almost daydreamy expression on his face. Smiling stupidly, he cracked his knuckles and took a lurching step forward.

"Okay," Tilley said, "fine, so you want to do this here. Well, at least let's—"

A little down the street, a porch light blinked on, a thick wedge of luminescent white flooding the front lawn. As one, the three witches turned their hosts' heads toward an opening door. Tilley glanced in the same direction and shook his head.

"What the heck is going on out here?" came a voice from the front door of the terrace. A semi-silhouetted figure stepped out into the light, tightening a thick belt around the waist of his dressing gown. The man was middle-aged and balding, his hair wet from a recent shower, his chest thickly thatched. The gown was crimson and his initials were emblazoned on the lapel in gold. He looked from the odd trio to Tilley and April and cocked his eyebrows, standing on the porch with his hands on his hips. "People're trying to sleep, you know."

"Go back inside," April called, stepping up beside the old witch hunter. "Please, just head back in. It's not safe out he—"

There must have been thirty feet of tarmac between the middle-aged man's lawn and the possessed dog-walkers, but the woman crossed it in a second. One moment she was standing beside her husband and the growling crossbreed; the next, she was a streak of dark autumnal colours lurching across the street. She flitted through the man's lawn gate and before April could blink, she was standing on his porch with her hand around his neck, spitting and snapping into his face. The man was hovering two feet off the ground; she was impossibly strong, and unnaturally fast, her scarf still fluttering around her neck when she began to squeeze.

"No!" Tilley yelled, lunging forward. In a flash the woman's husband appeared behind him, a whistle of cool air the only sign he had moved. The man grabbed him by the shirt and bellowed, launching Tilley across the street. Tilley yelled as he tumbled onto the kerb and rolled, scrambling desperately to his feet. Already the man who had thrown him was marching over.

"Shall I snap your neck?" the woman whispered softly, the man in the dressing gown wailing as his feet kicked blindly at the ground. "Or shall I turn your blood? Oh, I think so. It's so much *fun*…"

"Leave him out of this!" Tilley roared from across the street. It was no use; the dog-walking man lurched down and curled his fists around Tilley's coat lapels and heaved him into the road, throwing him like he was weightless. Tilley's head pounded as it hit the tarmac.

April watched in horror as the first witch dropped the middle-aged man onto the porch, where he crumpled to his knees. Gaping up at her with fear in his eyes, the man shook his head. Before he could open his mouth to beg for his life, the witch twisted her wrist and her eyes flashed a startling white.

The man screamed as his insides began to boil, mania flooding his blood as every cell in his veins sizzled, the veins themselves popping and snapping. He clutched at his chest, then his heart exploded in his ribs with a wet *thwop* and he gasped, swaying backward, red runnels leaking from his ears and nostrils.

Down the street, another light went on, a kitchen blind fluttering.

Tilley struggled to his feet, wiping blood off his lips with the back of his hand. Shoving the male dog-walker aside, he staggered across the street toward the woman, reaching into his coat. Behind him the man snarled, launching himself at Tilley and clamping his hand on the back of the old witch-hunter's head, slamming him forward. Tilley fell onto his front, face hitting the tarmac hard. He wheeled over onto his back to see the man bearing down on him, eyes wild and hungry, spittle flying from his mouth.

April had been frozen to the spot but suddenly her legs unlocked and she stumbled forward, eyes on the woman bathed in the porch light. The woman was laughing sickly as she watched her half-dressed victim cook from the middle, blood running in thick streams from his mouth and out of his eyes. He convulsed on the floor and April moaned, forcing herself forward.

The dog barked in her direction and her attention

was drawn to it. Her eyes widened. "Oh, shit," she whispered as the crossbreed leapt forward, eyes rabid and round, snout a mess of foam and blood. His teeth flashed as he lunged. April yelped and ducked out of the way, the crossbreed's jaws snapping shut inches from her neck. It went sprawling into the kerb and turned quickly, paws flattening on the ground as it pressed its muzzle low to the ground. Thick ropes of drool dangled from its maw. It pelted forward again.

"Kick it!" Tilley yelled, struggling inside his coat as the dog-walker launched a bony fist into his nose, splitting bone. The old man brought up a knee and it arced up into the witch's groin, doubling him over.

"I can't!" April screamed back, stumbling to the side as the dog pounced. Its shoulder barrelled into her ribs and she tumbled onto her back, rolling out of the way as it came at her again. In the corner of her eye she saw the dog's female owner marching toward them, a spray of blood decorating her autumn coat. April yelled as the dog slammed its paws down on her chest, reaching up with both hands to grab its muzzle and clamp it shut as it snapped and bit at her face. Drool spattered her face and neck as the thing growled, its snout hot and hairy, eyes flashing. "Fuck, I can't hurt it, it's a fucking dog!"

Another light came on down the street. Then another.

Tilley ducked between the witch's legs and

slammed an elbow into his back, sending him sprawling forward. He clocked the dog on April's chest, the woman heading for her, and whistled. The woman's head shot around and she glared at him.

Before he could yell the man had tackled him again and the tarmac rushed up into his face; he turned it at the last second, blood flying into his mouth from his broken nose. "Fuck!" he yelled as the hard ground grazed his cheek, the man-thing above him grabbing his left arm and twisting it behind his back. His right was still buried deep in his coat. She wasn't close enough…

April forced the dog off her with a burst of adrenaline-fuelled strength and it sprawled onto its back, rolling over quickly and launching itself at her again. She scrambled up, jumping as it swiped a paw at her shins, tumbling awkwardly over its back. "What the hell do we do?!"

Another porch flashed, another lawn flooded with light. She heard a door swing open.

"Bring it over here!" Tilley yelled, his voice muffled. She glanced over and saw him buried under the male dog-walker, then her eyes flitted up to the woman stalking toward them all. Her hands were spread, fingers straight and pointed, her face twisted into a cruel smile. April ran, tumbling toward the old witch-hunter, the dog at her heels.

"Then what?"

"Duck!" Tilley yelled, grabbing something hard and round from inside his coat and wrenching it free. The witch-woman descended on him, shoving her host's husband out of the way and grabbing Tilley by the throat. He felt hot, sharp claws rake his chest and yelled, blood spilling over his stomach. Then the woman clocked the thing in his hand and her eyes widened. "Fuck you," he gurgled, slamming the thing on the ground beside his head.

There was an explosion of anti-sound as the rock-shaped artefact shattered on the tarmac, shards of black flying between the old man's fingers. April yelled, covering her face, but her scream was sucked into the sudden void of silence that filled the world around her, a void that consumed every sound – the pounding of her heart, the pumping of blood in her ears, the snarling and snapping of the dog on her back – and turned it into… nothing. Then all the light was gone too and for a moment she was deep in the void, in a perfect sphere of absolute black, an absolute absence of light, of anything—

Then the sound and light returned and she heard herself screaming, tumbling onto her stomach. Behind her the dog slumped onto its back in the tarmac; before her, the man and woman crumpled, eyes rolling up in their heads, bodies suddenly still.

Tilley panted, looking over at her. His hand was shredded to ribbons, thick gashes of blood crisscrossing his palm and fingers. The tarmac was scorched black where he'd smashed the thing. "*Ow*," he muttered.

FORTIFY

"What the *hell* was that?!" April yelled, staggering to her feet. Around them, three bodies lay in the tarmac. The dog was on his side, a peaceful smile on the muzzle that had moments ago been champing at her throat, his eyes closed. The woman lay across her husband, blood on her coat, hair spread around her head like a halo. April's head pounded, the lights too bright, every sound too loud, like she had dropped into a vacuum then been shot violently out of it again. "Are they dead? Did you just kill them?"

"Deworming bomb," Tilley said, shaking his head as he climbed with some difficulty to his feet. "Forced them out of the hosts and back to wherever they came from."

"What about these three?" April said, leaning down to press two fingers against the dog's throat. "I can't feel anything. Am I supposed to? I don't know where a dog's pulse is."

"They're fine," Tilley said groggily, wiping his lip and chin. Blood was still running from his nose; he winced as his knuckle nudged the loose bone. "The deworming bomb is about the only thing that can remove witches without damaging the hosts. Anything in its radius. Sadly, its radius isn't very wide."

"Deworming bomb?"

"Yeah. It's like getting rid of—"

"Worms," April nodded disgustedly, "I get it. Like getting rid of tapeworms."

"Yeah."

"So they're going to be okay?"

"They'll wake up a little confused," Tilley said, looking around. At the far end of the street another light had come on; half the terraces were lit now, the people inside disturbed by the commotion. "They'll be fine. A little bruised, maybe."

"And the witches?"

"Elsewhere," Tilley said. "Not damaged, but I'd be surprised if they weren't a little hurt. It's a powerful thing, that. They won't bother us tonight, that's for sure."

"Great," April said, rising to her feet again. "Let's go use it on the others."

Tilley cocked an eyebrow, pointed to the scorch mark on the ground. "Single use," he explained, scratching the back of his head.

"You're not serious. You don't have any more?"

"They're hard to come by!" Tilley protested.

"That's the dumbest shit I've ever heard," April snapped. "You've got something that can do that, and you only brought one? And who came up with the name 'deworming bomb,' anyway?"

Tilley blinked sheepishly.

"You're kidding."

"Enough, anyway," he said, looking furtively around. "We have to get out of here. That's three down, but there's four left. Mother and three of her daughters."

"Her weird cult daughters."

"Weird *witch* daughters."

"So what else have you got in there?" April said, nodding to his coat.

"Trinkets," he shrugged. "Nothing as final as that. A few things that might help us to slow them down. Best I've got is a gun and a few magic bullets."

"Magic bullets?" April scoffed.

"Problem with that?"

"It's a little juvenile. Better than 'deworming bomb'."

He shook his head. "All I've got, anyway."

"But you've got a plan, right?"

"Get you out of here," Tilley nodded.

April looked down the street as another light flickered on. "Everyone else too?"

He shook his head. "The Parliament are only here for you," he said. "Everyone else is collateral. These things work in the shadows, always have. They'd rather keep this between us and them, but they'll burn through bodies like nothing else if they have to. If we stay here, they'll wipe out everyone in your town, including us. If we draw them somewhere else, then we'll be the only ones in danger."

"She seemed to enjoy it," April said, looking down at the unconscious woman. "She was laughing when she…"

"Mother isn't around to supervise," Tilley said grimly. "Let's say some of them are less strict about the rules than others. But if we can get away from here, then these people might be safe."

"Not us, though," April said quietly. "They're going to kill us, aren't they?"

Tilley looked at her for a moment, his expression dark and quiet. "They're going to try. We killed your aunt Coral. Clearly, she had connections; they're here for vengeance. I'll do everything I can to get you out of here, all right?"

"*You* came here to kill me," April said.

Some distance away, a voice called: "What's going on down there?"

Tilley nodded. "I'm a witch hunter," he said, "it's what I do."

"And now you're trying to help me."

"You're just a kid."

"And that matters, to people like you?"

"Apparently. Look, can we get out of here?"

"Hey!" someone yelled. "That's Anna down there! And Gary! Oi, you two, what have you done?"

Tilley backed up, looking around. Another light flicked on; another door swung open.

"They'll only hurt anyone who gets in their way," Tilley insisted. "You and me need to go. Now."

"You stay there!" came another voice. "Hogie, some old geezer's killed Gary's dog!"

"I'm calling the police!" an elderly woman yelled from right across the street.

"Fine," April whispered, looking toward the hillside. Above the village, the treeline was a dark, wide blotch of mismatched shapes. The pines were arrows spearing the moon; the slope was stained with shadow. "Let's go."

The two of them started toward an alley leading off the street, much to the elderly woman's disgust, ignoring her cries as they half-ran into the dark.

April led the way, running between houses and across the fields toward the woods at the edge of Black

Rope. Her mind spiralled as she tried to process everything that had happened, everything that *was* happening; it was useless. The two of them left the village behind and headed for the trees, almost running blind.

Behind them, three hooded creatures stalked forward from the shadows. Black cloaks fluttered in thin, moth-eaten folds around their hidden faces. One, the tallest, grinned behind its mask, an enormous stag skull with titanic antlers.

The three witches watched April and Tilley disappear into the forest. Behind them, a figure appeared from the direction of the street. "Hey! You three! What the hell is going on here?"

One of the creatures raised a withered hand, the fingers thrusting out of a loose, black sleeve. It clutched them together, claws clicking, and the shape behind them crumpled with a dull, wet *snap*.

"Permission to give chase, Mother," the witch with the bony mask whispered, eyes flashing yellow inside the stag's sockets.

"Permission granted," came the soft, slow voice of the Nora-thing. "Take your time, my daughters. Enjoy the hunt."

Soft needles blanketed the sloping earth, the pine boughs above still thick and full and dark. They had stopped in a clearing of sorts, the ragged edges punctuated with tall trunks that creaked loudly in the wind. The moon was high and full above them, and had seemed to hover there for hours; the night had been the longest April had ever experienced. She was exhausted, oddly hungry – her stomach had turned itself in knots, and she badly needed to pee but didn't want to venture into the deeper trees on her own – and every limb was on fire. She sat with her back pressed against a rugged trunk, her hands in her lap, watching Tilley's vague shape move through the trees beneath her.

She had pulled the book out of her jacket and it lay open at her feet, the pages scattered with dry brown needles. She had tried translating some of the pages but her head was swimming; she would have to stick with what she knew already. "What are you doing?" she called quietly.

Tilley looked up from the shadows, bent over by a knot of narrow trees twenty-or-so feet away. His bald head and hands were the only parts of him discernible from the shadows, his long coat obscuring the rest. She saw a smear of blood on his chin. "Trap," he replied simply, bowing his head again to focus on what he was doing. It looked like he was tying something around one of the spindly trees. As April watched, he tightened the wire, which glinted in the moonlight, then walked backwards with it to a nearby pine.

"A tripwire?" she said, cocking an eyebrow. "Fantastic."

Tilley said nothing, winding his wire around the pine tree before climbing up the slope on her right-hand side and looping it between the branches of another. It unspooled from a disc in his left hand; there seemed to be a good amount left. When he came to the next tree he bent down again, slipping his wire between two branches and fashioning a tight loop around them both. He was somewhere behind her shoulder when April spoke again.

"Your nose looks bad."

"It is," he supplied simply, moving to the next tree. He was forming a circle around the hillside clearing, thirty feet wide in every direction. The cable looked sharp.

April turned her head to look at him, his body bent around a thin stump on her left now. "What about the rest of it?" she said quietly. "Your scars."

He looked up briefly. When they locked eyes she saw something in the old man's expression that she hadn't noticed before: age. There was usually a sharpness in his eyes that seemed to have disappeared now; a spark that had been extinguished. The back of his bald head – now bruised from where the witch had grabbed him and slammed him into the road – was peppered with dots of scar tissue, and his left eye was surrounded by ragged splinters of white that screamed down through his cheek. And then there were the scars on the shelf of his jaw, claw marks raking his throat from Adam's apple to chin. They were thick and purple and old, but largely unhealed. They looked painful. With the broken nose and the blood on his chin starting to dry, he looked monstrous.

"You don't want to talk about them?" April guessed.

Wordlessly, Tilley stood up and moved to the last tree, unspooling another yard of wire and coiling it around the trunk.

"Fine," she shrugged, looking down into the open book. She opened her hand, reading silently, and flexed her fingers. Her palm tingled, and a tiny trace of green fire licked its way across her palm. She closed her fist and looked up again.

Tilley was winding the last of the wire around the spindly knot of trees where he'd started. She watched as he tied it around another branch, then dropped the spool into the knot. He looked up at her. Seemed to consider for a moment. Then he pointed, slowly, at his left eye. The explosion of scar tissue around it had painted the socket completely white. "Witch," he said flatly. "1980. Carver family called their local priest to come and exorcise their son. Priest died. The Agency got a call, and I took the case."

"You exorcised him?"

"The kid died," Tilley said, shaking his head.

"Parents were both possessed. The boy was, too, but he was just bait. The whole family were possessed by demons."

"I thought you said a witch did that to you."

"She did," Tilley sighed, walking up the slope toward her. He slumped down in the earth beside her, both of them looking downhill toward the village. She couldn't see his eye anymore; the one she could see was full of sorrow. "See, sometimes a demon and a witch will make a pact. Pacts like this have been vastly misunderstood through history, but they do exist. Turns out, all three demons had promised something to a witch, and failed to deliver. She happened to find them just after I did. She killed the boy first. Hung his body from a tree."

"Jesus."

"I got caught in the crossfire."

"What about this one?" April said, pointing vaguely to his chin. The three purple stripes glared angrily beneath his flesh.

"Werewolf," he said.

"You're kidding."

"I wish. No, that one stings."

"And what about… this?" April said, gesturing to the back of his head. Tilley's skin was pocked in dozens – hundreds – of places by those tiny white bumps, some bigger and more ragged than others.

He looked at her. Stiffly, after a minute, he said,

"Shotgun."

She cocked an eyebrow.

"I've got stomach cancer," he said. "Terminal. Bad. I found out… things got bad. I started drinking. Heavily. Got in a real bad way. Ended up in hospital. Lost my wife. Not her fault; I got nasty. Then I started to get *sick*. Real sick. Started treatment; didn't help. Made it worse. Made it unbearable."

"What happened?"

"I asked my son to kill me," Tilley said, looking blankly into the trees. "Abraham. I *begged* him. He said no, of course. But I'd lost everything. I felt awful. Elena – that's the chief up at the Agency – wouldn't let me work for a while. Said I was reckless. She had a point; I think I'd spent a year trying to get witches to kill me."

He smiled thinly.

"Didn't work. Guess I'm just too good at my job."

"Clearly."

"Anyway, I kept asking. He kept saying no, he wouldn't do it, wouldn't kill his own dad. Then things got worse, as they always do. I was dying, day by day, everything was painful… I begged, and pleaded, wore him down. *Really* wore him down. Finally, he said yes. Yes, he'd do it, put me out of my suffering. Guess I must have started to look really awful. I gave him the shotgun and sat down on a stool in the barn of an old abandoned farmhouse. I used to take him there to shoot clays. He stood behind me, pressed the barrel to the back of my head... I can still hear him crying. Me, too. Then... he staggered back, the barrel tipped up – bunch of shot raked the back of my head, not enough to put me down, just enough to put me in hospital."

"He backed out," April said.

Tilley looked at her, but didn't answer.

"I'm sorry."

"Extended stay in hospital started to put me right," he said. "Doctors found something new to try. Might keep me alive for *years*, they said. A couple, at least."

"How long ago was this?"

"Six years," Tilley said.

"You're better?"

"I've still got cancer."

"But you're not *dead*."

"No," he agreed, "I guess that's something."

"And what about your son?" she asked cautiously.

"Abe?" Tilley said, then he shook his head. Didn't say any more. There was something he wasn't telling her, she knew that much. But he had said enough.

"Why don't you retire? Stop hunting witches?" April said. "Christ, if you had, I'd be asleep right now."

Tilley smiled thinly, leaning his head back against the tree. "If I hadn't come for you, someone else would've. And some of the folks at the Agency wouldn't think twice about killing a kid."

"I'm not a kid," April said.

"You're younger than most witches."

"I'm not a *witch*," she insisted.

Tilley grinned. "Oh, you are. Could be a pretty good one, too."

April wrinkled her nose. "Aunt Coral was a witch. I'm not like her. Or those… things, stalking us."

"No," he said, "no, you're not. But you are a witch."

"Well, I don't want to be."

He shrugged.

"I only took the book to protect myself," April insisted. "I'm not like them. I'm… nice. I'm a nice person! I wouldn't possess anyone, I wouldn't hurt anyone, I'm not a tapeworm or whatever they are, I'm just… I'm just normal. Just me. I took that book because I didn't know what else to do with it."

"Maybe," Tilley said, "but you can *use* it because you're a *witch*. In your blood, I guess. I'd be useless with that book. But you've got the gift."

"Gift?"

"Whatever you want to call it. Natural ability. The witch itch."

"Doesn't feel like a gift."

"Not many things do. What can you do, anyway?"

"Simple stuff," April said. "I can shatter glass. Tried that one at the Catch Dog."

"The bottles," Tilley nodded.

"First time for everything. I can prepare a mean hex, but that won't help us very much now. I've been looking at this green fire thing, but I can't get more than a candleflame. I don't know how to turn blood, or anything. I might be able to turn them all into snakes, if I could remember the spell – but a snake is still pretty dangerous, so…"

"You're good, you know," Tilley said. "It's only the basics, but you're self-taught. Right? And I bet you don't understand half the languages in that book."

"I hardly understand one." April paused for a long time, then nodded toward the wire Tilley had wound around the clearing. "What does that do? You're not a witch, I get that, but you've got your coat full of magic objects. What's this one?"

He looked blankly at her. "It's a tripwire."

"Okay, but… what, is it going to turn them inside out? Like, you catch that with your toe and bam, you're a blackbird? Does it paint them purple, or—"

"That," Tilley said, "is a wire made from the fibres of Vinegar Tom's coat."

"Who?"

Tilley laughed. "You need to read up on your history of witchcraft."

"You could teach me."

His smile dropped.

"I didn't mean—"

"No, I know. But I can't. And you can't teach yourself, either. After this, after tonight, you have to destroy that book. Hide away somewhere and never use magic again.”

“Fine,” she said. Then, after a minute: “Why?”

“It’s not just witches and demons you have to worry about,” Tilley sighed. “People like me are going to come after you. They’re going to hunt you, for your whole life. Whether you use your magic or not. It’d help if you *didn’t*, but—”

“People from your agency?” April said. “Can’t you just… tell them not to hunt me?”

Tilley paused for a full minute. Together they looked into the trees. The shadows had begun to move. Finally, he said, “I don’t make it out of this one alive.”

His voice was quiet, dark.

“We’re going to find a way to stop the Parliament, I promise you that, but it’s going to take something big. It’s going to kill me.”

“You don’t know—”

“And it’s fine,” he said, ignoring her. “I’ll have done some good, so it’s okay. I’m going to get you out of this, April, but that’s the best I can do. After tonight, you’re on your own. And I wish you all the best, I really do. But I won’t be there to help.”

She looked at him for a long time, then nodded. “There is something else I can try. Magic I’ve been working on. I just don’t know if it’ll be any good.”

“Tell me about it.”

She did.

They watched the trees and waited.

THE PINES

April had begun to drift into a hazy kind of sleep when Tilley nudged her in the ribs. "Wake up," he muttered. "I'm sorry, kid. They're coming."

She blinked her eyes open, finding them bleary with… tears? She wiped them quickly and looked out into the trees. "I thought they'd find us quicker."

"They did," he said. "They've been watching us for a while."

She glanced up at him desperately, then looked back down the slope. She opened her mouth to ask Tilley if he thought they'd clocked the tripwire, but quickly saw that he was holding up a finger for silence. The witches could hear them, she realised. She swallowed.

It was impossibly dark, only the faintest traces of moonlight filtering through the silhouetted canopy. The wire was invisible from where April sat; she could only hope that the witches hadn't seen it either.

There were three of them, their shapes barely discernible from the trees. One of them was taller than the other two, and its head was all messed up. April couldn't quite figure out what was wrong with it, but it seemed too long, too angular, with a crown of some spiralling thorn-like arms sprouting from above its brow. All three wore long, dark robes – the other two had their hoods pulled up so that she couldn't see their faces – but there was something odd about the material. It was black and thick, but whenever the moonlight touched it the cloth flickered, becoming semi-transparent, revealing the withered, bony bodies beneath.

April shook her head. "What are they waiting—"

The witches advanced suddenly, all three of them lurching forward in a streak of shadow and bone. April yelped, overwhelmed by the sudden movement – from where she was sitting, it was like the entire forest had unfurled at once and every speck of darkness had spilled out of it toward her – and scrambled to her feet, hurling her back against the tree. Beside her Tilley was already up, and before she could stumble forward he held out a hand to keep her back. "The wire," he said, "any second—"

There was a piercing *hiss* as the first witch hit the tripwire, the sound of steak sizzling in a pan of oil that's been on the heat for far too long. Rather than heat, though, April felt a surge of cold air flood the forest. The treetops above them whistled as a gust of air blasted upward; by now the second witch had flitted into the wire too, and for a horrifying moment April saw them caught in the thing, which was glowing a bright, furious white. The third witch hung back, apparently having caught on a little quicker than the second.

The wire flickered in shades of electric white and blue, the two witches glued to it like flies to sticky paper. Their bodies convulsed and April screamed at the horrifying vision, able to see them much more clearly now that lightning was coursing through the tripwire: the first was a faceless thing in a black, billowing cloak, its shrieking bony mouth visible in the dark shadow cast by its hood. Teeth flashed. The second witch was taller, its robes flitting in and out of reality to expose the crooked shape beneath; this one wore the stag's skull, its sockets flaring, the crown of antlers thrusting out of its head creaking and twisting as the creature heaved itself, finally, from the wire.

"Get down," Tilley muttered, and April saw something in his hand. Her eyes widened as he raised the revolver, pointing it at the third witch.

"The others!" April yelled. The second witch had pulled itself from the wire and the two of them were straightening, evidently only briefly disarmed by the trap. Lightning still flickered across the razor wire.

"Tom's dealing with them," Tilley said quietly, and he squeezed the trigger.

The revolver exploded and April backed up, slamming her hands over her ears. A perfectly-aimed bullet punched into the third witch's chest, blowing her back into the trees. Red fog poured out of the wound and billowed upward. The creature screamed, its robes disappearing for a full second to reveal the writhing, skeletal thing within. Tilley fired again, again, the second and third bullets striking the witch in the shoulder and neck. It surged forward, blood-red mist blooming from all three wounds and forming smoke trails in the air. The bullets seemed to have hurt the creature but it came forward nonetheless, unfazed, and April yelped as it leapt easily over the tripwire and landed, sprawling, on its hands and knees in the dirt not twenty feet from them.

It was then that she saw Tom.

The wire thrummed and a thin white smoke-shape unfolded from it, exploding into the night and roaring. At first it was made entirely of mist, the shape within folding and unfolding, haunches shuddering as its guts solidified – then it clarified into something more, something powerful – its fur painted with the grey strokes of fog but its insides, visible through translucent hide, punctuated with smears of gory red and purple. A muscular, shaggy dog lunged toward the first two witches, the ones that had touched the wire, and April watched with wide eyes as the beast snapped its foggy jaws hungrily.

Made from the fibres of Vinegar Tom's coat, he had said.

Well, she supposed that was Vinegar Tom.

"What do I do?" April yelled.

"Whatever you can!" Tilley yelled back, squeezing the trigger again. The revolver pumped out a fourth bullet with a titanic boom and it smashed into the third witch's kneecap, buckling it. It screeched and pulled itself back onto its feet, red mist pouring from its leg and chest as its eyes burned electric yellow.

"She's not going down!" April screamed.

"I know!" Tilley said, firing a fifth bullet. It pulped the witch's neck and its head rolled back, then tipped forward again. A writhing sheet of bloody fog rolled out of its throat as it grinned and lunged at him.

"How many magic bullets did you have?"

"Six!" Tilley yelled, firing the last one.

It smacked the witch right in the eye.

The creature howled as its bony face exploded inward, red fog shooting out of its mouth in a horrifying spiral and curling into the treetops. It twitched violently, both arms shooting out to the side, knees crumpling beneath it as it sunk into the earth. The creature sprawled on its front and twitched, body sizzling. "Ha! Suck that, you creepy bitch!"

April wheeled around to watch the ghostly form of Vinegar Tom pounce at the stag-headed witch's chest, launching it into the ground. The robed thing reached up and grabbed the snarling dog by both shoulders, wrenching it off with ease. Tom bellowed, clamping his jaws around the second witch's arm as it raked its bony fingers at him. The witch drew back sharply and Tom snapped his head around to the stag-skulled creature again, pounding one paw into the ground as he prepared to leap. Then he leapt.

The witch lowered its head and swung, and Vinegar Tom yelped with agony as the thick antlers of the stag slid easily into his semi-visible organs. Ichor sprayed from the wounds and dissipated in the air as the ghostly dog vanished.

As one, the witches turned their heads toward the clearing.

"Shit," Tilley said, dropping the gun. The third witch smouldered at his feet.

"I've got this," April whispered, stepping forward. She raised both hands and whispered something under her breath. Tilley watched uncertainly as the two witches advanced, stepping easily over the tripwire. It flickered uselessly.

"Careful..."

April's eyes flashed a bright, neon green and thick tendrils of flame shot out of her hands.

"Jesus!" Tilley yelled as streams of green fire exploded into the trees, wildly missing both witches and lighting the lower branches of a single pine tree. The flame was intense and bright, and Tilley felt the heat in his entire body. It hurt. The fire streamed forward for a minute, illuminating the whole forest, bright enough to blind him, then it died as quickly as it had come. The afterglow crackled.

The witch with the stag skull took a step forward, unbothered.

"Go again," Tilley breathed, dipping a hand into his coat and pulling out a sharp, serrated knife. Like that of the Undoing Knife, the handle was made of bone; unlike the Undoing Knife, the blade glowed a crackling blue.

April grinned and her eyes flared again as she punched her right hand forward and a swirling, angry pillar of green fire streamed out of it, shooting toward the witch with the stag skull—

It fizzled out pathetically as the witch raised both of its hands, skeletal fingers splayed outward, eyes flashing red. April yelped as the fire recoiled violently, a furious rope of green shooting back into her palm. She clutched her hand and staggered back.

"It's okay," Tilley said, stepping forward and brandishing the knife. "You get away from her!"

Stag Skull looked at him. It hardly moved a hand; April caught a flash of bony nail, then Tilley's body went sailing back into the tree. His back smacked the bark with a crunch and he fell. "Shit!"

"I'm fine," he yelled. "Just get out of here!"

April looked from Stag Skull to the other witch and swallowed. The one wearing the skull ignored her completely, lurching in Tilley's direction; the other grinned beneath its hood and came for April.

"Shit," she said again, staggering back.

The witch raised both hands and its eyes flashed blue in the shadow of its hood. Just out of her field of view, there was a grunt as Stag Skull grabbed Tilley by his coat and heaved him off the ground.

April turned and ran.

The witch followed her into the woods, moving easily through the shadows. April staggered under hanging branches, almost tripping more than once, struggling uphill away from the village. In the distance, she heard Tilley yell in pain; she couldn't help him, not right now. She had her own problems to—

The witch swiped at her back, bony fingers raking her between the shoulderblades. April screamed and fell onto her hands, rolling onto her back just in time to see the witch shooting a bolt of blue electricity out of its palm. April shrieked, rolling to the side. The lightning bolt smashed into the ground where she had been, producing a crater of scorched black earth. The creature laughed, an awful sound like a death rattle.

"Mine," it rasped, splaying its fingers as it advanced, leaning down to lay a hand on the girl's cheek. The fingers clicked as the creature ran its hand up the side of her skull, finally settling its palm on her temple. The other hand clamped the other temple and April moaned as that blue light flashed in the witch's eyes again. It was going to fry her brain.

Or not.

"You know what sound a teenager makes when it's boiled from the inside?" the witch wheezed, grinning with bony teeth. Then it plumbed both of its clawed thumbs into April's ears, the sharp points jamming deep into the canals within. "It sounds like thi—"

April grinned.

The witch paused. "What are you..."

April winked, then closed both of her eyes. Her body flickered, traces of purple mist surrounding her, enveloping her.

Then she disappeared.

The witch stumbled forward, hands almost clapping together as it hit its knees in the dirt. It whirled around – too slow.

April stood over the witch, smiling thinly. Her eyes shone purple. "Didn't know if I could do it," she whispered, flexing her fingers. "Do you know how hard it is to be in two places at once? Thank *god* it worked."

The smile dropped. The purple turned to a violent, fiery green.

"Die," she whispered, then emerald flames exploded from her hands and punched into the witch's face. The bony thing screamed as fire surged all around it, rolling out of April's palm in stream after stream. The smell of burning meat rose into the air as the thing's body began to broil.

Eventually April stopped, the light in her eyes flickering. She doubled over, clutching her belly. Her hand was warm, but not unpleasantly so. For a moment she stood with her eyes closed, catching her breath. Then she straightened, drew a deep breath in, let it out again.

The witch was a shrivelled, black husk at her feet.

Somewhere behind her, Tilley screamed.

April staggered back into the clearing and froze.

The witch with the stag's skull loomed over Tilley, both its hands raised, whirling rings of black smoke dancing in thick coils around its fingers. Its antlers were slick with blood, its clawed fingers too. It was laughing.

Tilley was on his back in the dirt, coat splayed out behind him. The knife with the blue blade was lodged in his side, blood pooling from it. His stomach had been gored, the shirt shredded to ribbons, the damage impossible to discern through a mess of softly-pumping viscera. His face and neck were bloody, his ankle bent at an awkward angle. Panting, he reached for the knife and winced as he unsheathed it from his own meat, pointing it shakily at the witch's chest. The blue glow had faded. Fresh blood sprayed from the now-open wound.

"Hey!"

The witch turned its head, ropes of red flung from its antlers. It pointed a hand toward April and the swirling cloud of black seemed to pulse as it whispered something. April's eyes widened and she raised her own hand – just in time. A jet of inky black shot toward her face and her eyes flickered green, a wall of neon flame erupting into view before her. Green and black collided and burst outward in a shower of smouldering sparks. The witch growled.

"You should not have come back here," the creature rasped.

"Back where?" April said from behind it.

The creature wheeled around, robes billowing, and saw the girl standing ten feet away in the opposite direction. The witch looked back – the first April was still there, tiny traces of flickering purple curling around her body. Two of them. The witch turned to the second April – purple wisps of smoke threaded around this one's arms, too – and snarled.

"Advanced magic," the witch leered. "You'll tear yourself apart."

Then it roared, spreading its arms, both wrists twisting violently, simultaneously. Twin pillars of swirling black smoke exploded toward the two Aprils, inky jets of shadow snatching and grabbing at the air. As one, the Aprils raised their hands and a wall of green fire flickered into existence in front of each one, blocking out the shadow.

The witch laughed. "How long do you think you can keep this up? How much strain your body is undertaking to double yourself like this?"

"Triple," a third April whispered, sneaking into view from behind the tree and grabbing the blue-bladed knife from Tilley's blood-soaked hand. She lunged forward and thrust it deep into the witch's stomach, bellowing with anger as she drove it up into the creature's ribs.

The witch looked down at her, dumbfounded, and just for a moment April saw terror in the eyes buried deep in the dark, black pits of the stag's eye-sockets. She smiled. The witch's arms fell, the black smoke vanishing into nothing, and either side of the creature a thick, green tendril of fire surged forward, consuming its body.

Stag Skull shrieked as April forced the serrated blade upward, carving a deep track through its ribs.

Black blood sprayed out and splashed her face and April yelled, punching her hand into the witch's chest. She found what she was looking for and yanked it out of the hole she'd made, stumbling back with the knife still in her hand, the blade soaked black.

Either side of her, the other Aprils disappeared.

The witch crumpled to its knees and tipped backward.

April gazed at the heart for a second, a dreadful shrivelled thing, thick black veins crisscrossing it like electric cables. It beat once, twice, then stopped.

She tossed it into the ground.

"April…" Tilley whispered behind her.

She dropped to the ground and looked him over, breathing hard as the mania started to leave her veins, quickly folding her palm over the wound in his side. "What do I do?"

"I'll be fine," he breathed. "You ever cauterised a wound?"

"Of course I haven't."

"You're about to learn. Hey, listen…"

A dribble of blood seeped out of his mouth. April nodded, tears blearing her eyes.

"That was fucking fantastic," he smiled weakly.

She laughed, relief flooding her chest. Behind them, the witch with the stag skull had begun to smoulder. "I know," she said.

"Now," Tilley said, laying his hand over hers and

pressing it firmly against his side. "This is going to hurt me more than it hurts you."

B.W.F.A.

Mother crawled through the girl's veins, writhing and twisting.

The Nora-creature hung in the air over the vicarage roof, hands spread by her sides, feet dangling. The child's hair blew in her face, her good eye flickering white. The other was a gory crater. Thick plumes of deep, red fog swirled around the old building, buckling and folding and unfolding and whispering as they spiralled in dense bloody circles beneath her.

The witch smiled as two shapes appeared at the edge of the woods.

Tilley walked stiffly, clutching his side, one arm

draped heavily over April's shoulders. The teenager's stomach was painted glossy red and her face was sprayed with blood, but she looked largely unharmed; the old man, however, was on his last legs. Together they hobbled downhill, Tilley's eyes locked on the vicarage, his lips pressed firmly shut despite the pain.

She watched them come. Beneath her the vicarage windows flashed red and white, neon pulses detonating the fog outside. Suspended six feet above the sagging roof, the Nora-thing closed her hands into tiny fists. A wisp of faint white light leaked from the slimy hole of her left eye. The right flashed brightly. The fog was chewing at the edges of the house, swirling chunks of brick and stone sucked outward into the slow whirlwind. The vicarage was falling apart. Where holes had been ripped from the walls, streams of electric light flared out like blood winging from holes.

"Step back," Tilley said quietly as they reached the bottom of the hill and approached the vicarage. Behind them the forest was impossibly dark, a silhouette of pointed spears against the pinkish sky. Dawn was coming. Not fast enough. He reached up to his collar. "Remember what I said, April. Get out of here. Look after yourself."

April grabbed his arm before the old man could move forward. "Stop it," she hissed. "You can't—"

Tilley shook his head, tugging his arm out of her grip. Sharply, he tugged at something hanging around his neck. It came loose and fell into his palm, a thin glinting chain draping between his fingers. "It's time," he said.

April watched helplessly as he turned his head toward the vicarage and looked up, stepping closer to the red storm.

"My daughters," the Nora-thing called loudly, a dark gurgling undertone clinging unnaturally to the child's lilting, almost-singsong voice. "What of them?"

"You know," Tilley said. He winced as pain rocked through him, nearly crumpling. There was blood in his mouth. His ankle was ruined, his stomach burning. "You can feel it, can't you?"

Slowly, the Nora-thing smiled. "No matter. The Parliament will reform. Less can be said of you. You're going to die tonight, old man."

"Make it quick," he said. "Sun's coming up."

A flicker of anger crossed the child's face. She stood in the air thirty feet above them, a looming silhouette with her blustering hair haloed by the oncoming light. Slowly, the child turned her head toward April. The smile reappeared. "Did he tell you?"

April swallowed.

"Don't," Tilley warned her. "Don't engage. Not now. Whatever she says, it's not—"

"He didn't," the witch smiled. "Would you like to know what really happened to his son?"

April frowned.

Tilley glared up at the Nora-thing. "This isn't important."

"You asked him to kill you," April said. "He was about to, then he pulled the gun at the last second. The shot grazed the top of your head. That's what you told me."

"That's all that happened." Tilley called up to Mother: "Is this really important? Honestly?"

"Might be," the Nora-thing shrugged. The child grinned maliciously. To April: "Wouldn't you like to know why he pulled the gun?"

"He backed out," April said quietly, shaking her head. Glanced at Tilley. "Just decided… he couldn't do it. Right?"

"Right," Tilley said, seething. In an attempt to change the subject, he raised his fist, the necklace clenched inside. "Enough—"

"He was killed," the witch growled. Her smile was thin and the words trickled with hate. "Your friend here has butchered a lot of witches, girl. And witches have sisters. Brothers. We look after our kin. We *avenge*."

"Stop," Tilley snarled.

"Abraham was about to pull the trigger," the witch continued. "Wasn't he? He didn't have second thoughts. Didn't have a single qualm about killing you. The man who raised him. He'd been *waiting* for a chance to end your life. And then you offered it to him.

And he *relished* it."

"Stop it."

"Then one of my daughters found you both, in that barn. You never heard her coming. Did you? Didn't know she'd come at all, until she snuck up behind you both and ripped poor Abraham's heart out through his spine—"

"—*Stop it!*—"

"—*That's* why he missed, girl. *That's* why the old man has these scars. Because the son paid for the father's sins."

April swallowed again. "Why does this—"

"Because since that day," the Nora-thing said, her face suddenly serious, the socket around her missing eye going terribly dark, "he has killed *hundreds* of our kind. *Our* kind, girl. Not mine. Ours. You understand? He is the enemy here, not me. He has slaughtered and butchered and defiled and violated and plundered—"

"Wouldn't you?" Tilley whispered, and April wasn't sure if he was talking to her or Mother.

"He was going to kill *you*, remember. And when he's done with me, he will."

April froze.

"Oh, yes," Mother smiled. "That's the plan, isn't it, old man? Use the girl's basic magic until you've spent us all, and then take her out too?"

Tilley glanced back. "I'm not—"

April's eyes were dark.

Above them both, the Nora-thing laughed bitterly, maniacally. The red fog swirling around the vicarage blossomed, more and more hunks of debris shooting out of the sides of the building and joining the whirling, writhing throng.

"Join us," Mother whispered. "Help me to kill him, girl, and be the first member of my new Parliament. You have the potential for great magic. I could teach you so much. You could be so powerful."

"Don't listen to her," Tilley said.

"Shut up."

"That's right," Mother smiled, "take control, girl. You have displayed such mastery of the simple spells. Imagine what you could do with training, with resources, imagine how *celestial* you could become…"

"That's enough!" Tilley roared suddenly, limping forward and opening his hand. The chain was wrapped around his wrist; the necklace itself dropped a few inches, then came to rest just beneath his fist. It glinted purple. April stared. The Nora-thing seemed to pause. "You know what this is?"

Mother said nothing.

It looked like a locket, but the gem in the centre was enormous and perfectly round, a crystal with a swirling purple vortex inside.

"What is that?" April whispered.

"Last resort," Tilley said. He yelled up at the floating witch: "You know, don't you?"

"You wouldn't," Mother hissed.

The purple gem swung gently from his hand. Bright spangles of pink glittered in its centre. "I'm dying," he said. "I would."

"I know who killed him," Mother offered. "Your son. I could tell you."

"You think I don't know?"

The Nora-thing looked desperately at April. "Join me. Kill him."

April blinked. Stepping forward, she said, "What is it?"

Tilley clenched his jaw. "It's a Tunnel Stone." He grinned. "Another one of my stupid names. But it does what it says. It's like a wormhole. A tunnel waiting to split open, with one destination at the end."

"Where?"

"I open it up," Tilley said, "and it sends her to Hell." He paused.

Then, quietly, he said, "And me with her."

"So do it," Mother screeched, spreading her arms suddenly. Red fog clouded around her. "Do it, you coward!"

Tilley looked at April and smiled sadly. "See you round," he said. He pressed his thumb to the Tunnel Stone.

"Kill him!" Mother shrieked, good eye blazing white. "Join me, girl, kill him!"

Tilley stepped forward. "Enough," he said. "Time

for me and you to go on a little trip, honey."

He was closing his thumb around the stone when April grabbed him by the collar and yanked him back. "Don't," she whispered, eyes flashing darkly, then her fist shot forward and smashed him in the nose.

Tilley cried out as blood flooded his mouth, tumbling onto his back. Pain shot into his skull, a feeling like his brain turning to pulp as warmth streamed down his throat. The necklace fell from his hand and he looked up desperately. "What are you doing?"

"Excellent," Mother whispered, offering a spindly hand. "Come, girl, join me—"

"Shut the fuck up!" April yelled. She glanced down at him. "I'm sorry about your nose."

"What did you do?" Tilley said weakly, blood bubbling from his mouth as he tried to scramble onto his feet. He fell, leg crumpling under him.

April glanced toward the village. He followed her gaze and saw dark shapes trickling across the horizon, heading toward them. Tilley squinted through a haze of blood and crimson fog and swallowed.

"You know those simple spells you were talking about?" April called up to the witch, pointing to direct Mother's attention toward the high street as a stream of sunlight beaded on the distant trees. April looked down at Tilley and grinned. "I called for help."

The first Jeep pulled up with a scream, handbrake-turning into position just outside the vortex of swirling blood-fog. Above the vicarage, the thing in the child's body glanced down at the black military vehicle and snarled. A second and third pulled up the other side of the building as the doors of the first swung open, the three vehicles forming a remarkably even triangle around the vicarage. Five or six more cars pulled up quickly, forming a line beyond the foggy ring that April couldn't quite see. The air was thick with the stink of petrol fumes and the roaring of engines; still, she heard the soldiers yelling as they leapt from the Jeeps and got into formation.

"Insolent husks!" the Nora-thing shrieked, drawing April's attention back up to her. Her eyes widened as the creature streaked forward suddenly, body becoming a blur as it shot down from the roof toward her. April screamed as the thing raised both of Nora's hands mid-pounce, lips pulling back in a fierce growl, eyes flashing blood-red as streams of poisonous red mist shot out of her palms.

"No!" Tilley yelled, suddenly in front of her, shoving her back. April yelled as a thick, fast tendril of smoky red punched into the old man's chest, knocking him back a pace. He roared defiantly as more of the blooming mist swept into his stomach, gorging on him.

He ground a heel into the earth and howled with pain, head tipped back, the witch laughing menacingly above him as whorls of crimson ricocheted off his body and blossomed into a cloud of recoiling snake-like fingers. She smelled blood and burning and lunged forward – then, in the corner of her eye, she saw a soldier in black fatigues signalling for her to stay back. A dozen of them had formed a ring around them now, visors down so their faces were hidden, shoulders and chests covered with thick black plates.

"Now!" yelled a female voice somewhere in the chaos. Red plumes of fog were screaming from every window of the vicarage, half of the walls crumbled away, bricks and mortar swirling violently in the bloody miasma. Amid the plasma and the stink of charred flesh, the Nora-thing cackled maniacally, shooting more and more bolts of dense fog into Tilley's chest, ripping him apart.

At once, three of the soldiers stepped forward. April's eyes widened as she saw what looked like cannons in their arms: thick black cylinders, their barrels etched with dozens of runes that glowed a sinister yellow. On the unseen woman's command they fired, ethereal projectiles shooting out of each cannon and triangulating on the floating witch-creature in the middle of it all.

April hurtled backward as the three projectiles connected.

She screamed as a wave of energy washed over her, raising both hands to protect her face and looking up through her fingers as Tilley was blown into the grass beside her. His chest was a ragged mess of bloody flesh, his stomach similarly ripped to shreds. He wasn't moving, his eyes jammed shut. April looked up in awe.

Surrounded by soldiers, the Nora-thing hung in the air, twelve feet high, screaming.

From each cannon, a thick black chain punched into the air and looped around the creature's body. The chains were eerily translucent, flickering and clarifying ghost-like, but they looked strong, each angular link the size of a fist. Wrapped in dozens of loops of the incorporeal black chains, the witch-thing writhed and squirmed, arms pressed against her sides, good eye flashing every colour: black then red, then yellow, green, blue, lightning streaming from her face—

"Eject!" yelled the unseen woman. Now April noticed that every soldier was pointing what looked like a semi-automatic rifle at the thing in Nora's body. Her eyes widened as, all at once, they squeezed the triggers.

A dozen projectiles shot into the vicinity of the creature and it screamed as they exploded into a fine orange mist, enveloping the thing. Nora's head shot back and her mouth yawed open. April screamed, terrified, as Mother poured out of her.

The witch punched both clawed fists out of Nora's mouth first, then the spindly arms appeared, raking at the air. The thing's skin was the same burnt grey as the others; impossibly it was crowning, its bald skull exploding from Nora's mouth as the hands came down to lock around the girl's shoulders, elbows pointed up at insane angles. The creature screeched, its bony chest surging out of Nora's unhinged jaw, eye-sockets blaring with a dimming red light. Then, before its legs could appear, it exploded into a shower of bloody gobs, viscera launching itself in every direction.

All at once, everything stopped.

The chains flickered out of existence and Nora's body plummeted toward the ground, where a waiting soldier caught her gently. The orange fog was fading fast, two or three soldiers already rushing to Tilley's side to cover his chest and stomach with what looked like plastic packages of cool blue fluid. April felt herself fading, the mania finally shrivelling in her veins, and black fog clouded her vision as she began to pass out. She tipped back, waking violently in the moment before she hit the ground, sprawling on her back and suddenly horribly, dreadfully alert.

The thick red vortex of red fog had gone, and there was a nightmarish convulsion of sound as all the swirling stone and brickwork dropped to the ground, forming a ring of debris around the damaged vicarage. Then that, too, began to collapse, the ruins no longer held in place by the witch's magic, every cell of the building dropping into the earth in a plume of billowing dust. A crashing cacophony boomed up the hillside, filling every one of April's senses. Panting, hardly able to hear over the thumping of blood in her ears, April moaned and turned her head. One soldier slid a long needle into Tilley's throat while another bandaged his neck, two more clamping his body to the earth as it fitted and seized,

A blurry figure swung into view. April looked up, senses swimming. A pair of polished black shoes, size five or six, then above those, black tights and a sharp, pleated skirt. Grey.

Elena Fox stood above April, one hand on her hip, her grey blazer fluttering in the breeze. A peach-coloured blouse was spattered with blood. Clipped brown hair flew around her face as she looked down at the girl in the grass.

"Nora…" April whispered.

"She'll be fine," Elena nodded. "She may have a broken jaw, but she's about to receive the best medical help the country can offer. The Agency will deal with any resulting traumas. We won't be able to fix the eye, I'm afraid."

"She's going to live?"

"Oh, yes," Elena smiled thinly. She glanced back at Tilley. "So will he, if I have anything to say about it. He's got a lot to answer for."

April smiled, blinking out the bleariness. Her heart was pounding. She started to sit up, opening her mouth to thank the woman. Then she froze.

At some point, a long-barrelled revolver had appeared in Elena Fox's hand. April was looking right down the barrel, a long black tunnel at the end of which, she was quite sure, was what Tilley had called a magic bullet. The gun itself was ancient, etched with runes like the cannons the soldier had used.

"As for you," Elena said, "you're coming with me."

LOCKUP

ONE WEEK LATER

The corridor was long and dark, the concrete floor painted a smeared, unpleasant white, the walls left bare and lit only with the swinging amber haloes of sconces hanging from the ceiling. It had once been a tunnel connecting two underground stations; now both were abandoned and the tunnel disused, the whole network owned by the British Witch Finders Agency for purposes which were not entirely documented.

Tilley coughed as he followed the soldiers, limping

awkwardly along the concrete behind them. His left leg was fitted with a vice-like brace, his weight pressed onto one crutch which clicked with every jangling step. The skin grafts had begun, though he still needed a few surgeries. He had been told to rest. Officially, he hadn't yet been discharged from the hospital.

"Just in here," the first soldier said, turning and pressing her back to the wall beside one of the many steel doors. A heavy wheel, like one you might find on a submarine bulkhead, exploded from the centre of the door. Slowly, Tilley hobbled toward it. The second soldier stood the other side of the door. Both of them brandished semi-automatic rifles, the barrels engraved with arcane script. Their visors had been raised as they headed down the tunnel; now, as the second soldier started to turn the wheel with an enormous clanking rattle, they both pulled them down to cover their faces.

The door swung open. Glancing once at each guard for confirmation, Tilley stepped into the cell.

"Hello," he said quietly.

The room was tiny and intensely claustrophobic, perhaps seven feet by seven, with a single fluorescent light flickering in a strip along the walls. Inside were a low, thin bed and a vacuum toilet, and a bookshelf upon which April had been allowed to place three books and a single stuffed teddy. Along the side of the teddy's gut, a line of very obvious black stitching told Tilley that the toy had been thoroughly investigated.

The walls were carved with titanic runes and symbols, anti-witchcraft signs painted in salt and brine on the concrete. Clumps of moss gathered in the corners of the room where faint fluorescent light lingered in flickering pools. A gaming console had been arranged uncomfortably close to the toilet, the socket where it was plugged in encased in concrete so that the wires could not be meddled with.

April looked up. She sat against the far wall, her eyes dark, her body hunched into an angular ball. She glared bitterly at Tilley.

"I've been trying to get you out of here," he said quietly, stepping further into the cell and crouching painfully. His chest was healing slowly, most of the ragged scars on his body sealed and stitched up but threatening to split open again if he expended himself too much. His insides seemed to be boiling. "I really have, April. I'm working on it."

She cocked an eyebrow, glancing past him to the guards, both of whom stood firmly in the doorway.

Tilley nodded toward the games console. The cartridge slot was soldered closed. "What have you got in there, Tetris?"

Still nothing. Her gaze returned slowly to him, but her expression didn't change. The girl's face was solidly hateful.

Tilley sighed. "You know, I really am… they'll listen, in the end. I just need to…" He scratched the back of his neck anxiously. Leaning on the crutch, he swung his head around to look back. "You two, could we have a minute alone?"

The guards looked at each other.

He grinned weakly. "Come on. You've strip-searched me already."

Without a word, the guards turned and stepped out into the tunnel, pulling the door to. Tilley waited for a moment, then heard the wheel rattle.

Turning back to April, he glanced down at her hands. They were folded in her lap. "How long can you hold this up?" he whispered.

April paused, then raised a hand so he could see. Her fingers were purple and foggy, the tips almost invisible.

"A little longer," she said. Her eyes tracked the old man's wounds down to his stomach. "Long enough, I hope. How are *you* doing?"

"I'll be fine," Tilley said with a vague wave. He hesitated. "I'd come and find you, you know. But they'd follow me if I did. You're too powerful. When they find out you're not in here, they *will* come after you."

"That's all right," she said. The fingers of both hands flickered, faint trails of wispy purple fog swirling between them. "I'll be far enough away by the time they do."

"But if you ever need me—"

"I know," April said. She smiled. "Same to you, fella."

Eight-hundred miles away, the young girl sat in a ragged fray of glass overlooking the sea, a chalk-white cliff face plunging away beneath her dangling legs. The sunlight was pleasantly warm and the long grass swung about her as a soft breeze came in from the ocean. She smiled. The book was tucked into a rucksack in the grass by her side, the zip pulled tight. On the horizon, a slow fishing vessel made its glacial journey from one tiny sandbank to another.

"Are you safe?" Tilley said, back in the cell.

April nodded, looking out to sea. She could feel the cell around her, feel Tilley's presence, just about see him in her mind's eye. Enough to keep the illusion going, for now. "I'm safe," she said. "I'm good. All things considered."

Her smile grew as the soft wind brushed her neck. Powerful magic stirred in her chest.

"I'm really, really good."

<u>A NOTE FROM THE AUTHOR</u>

Thank you for reading *Parliament of Witches*. As an independent author every single person reading my work is so valued and I can't express how much your time means to me. For more of my books, follow me on Instagram @heath_horrorwriter or check out my website derekheathhorror.com where I'll keep you updated on future releases.

I hope you enjoyed! If so, please leave a review on Amazon if you can. I'd love to know what you thought.